Raksha(si)

The Beginning

DEEPTI POTNIS

INDIA • SINGAPORE • MALAYSIA

ISBN 979-8-89133-966-8

Raksha(si) - The Beginning

Deepti Potnis

Table of Contents

Prologue....4
Chapter 1 – Veena....8
Chapter 2 – Disaster strikes....16
Chapter 3 – Mr. Green eyes....23
Chapter 4 – Dark Musings....34
Chapter 5 – Mr. Khanna....36
Chapter 6 – Family matters....45
Chapter 7 – Parampara Designs....52
Chapter 8 – Date night....62
Chapter 9 – Funeral....72
Chapter 10 – Dark Musings....85
Chapter 11 – Inheritance....87
Chapter 12 – Money & other matters....94
Chapter 13 – Nemina....102
Chapter 14 – Family dinner....119
Chapter 15 – The attack....130
Chapter 16 – Maya....138
Chapter 17 – The haunted cottage....148
Chapter 18 – Raghu....156
Chapter 19 – Spells....167
Chapter 20 – The kiss....171

Chapter 21 – Malevolence..180

Chapter 22 – Another victim 188

Chapter 23 – Revelations..193

Chapter 24 – Dark Musings 200

Chapter 25 – The trap...202

Chapter 26 – Immortality 206

Epilogue 216

Acknowledgements 219

Prologue

15 years ago...

Gaurav & Lokesh needed a girl. The younger the better. They were once again in debt & this time simple theft would not get them the money they needed to square it off & get their next drug fix. This was an option that Rekha mavshi (aunt) had given them. Sell her a girl & she would pay them handsomely. With the recent police raids & the advent of mobile phones, her business was suffering for want of fresh meat. It would be simple enough. They just had to case a nearby school & snatch one of the girls when no one was looking.

Gaurav had bought some expensive chocolates & was waiting at a distance from the school gate while Lokesh had hidden behind a tree inside the school compound before the school let out. With his prominent scar & pan stained teeth, Lokesh would not have gone unnoticed but Gaurav had taken special care with his appearance. He had worn clean clothes & brushed his hair as well. As the school let out the girls came out in hordes. The mothers had come to pick up the younger girls while some of the older ones left in groups. Gaurav was careful to not approach any of them. Finally, once the school was relatively empty, there was just one child left. A girl of about 7-8 yrs. was sitting inside the school veranda eating her snacks. She had curly brown hair & big brown eyes with fair skin. Gaurav was sure that she would fetch a handsome price.

After casing the school for a week this was the girl Gaurav had decided they would take. She always left a little late with her sister who was a few years older. Today was no different. Gaurav carefully approached the girl

"Your mother has sent me to pick you up. Your sister will be staying in school later than usual. She has one more extra class. I will take you home." He said with a smile. "Look she even sent your favorite chocolate" he said offering her the chocolate.

The girl gave him a sweet smile & shook her head. "It's ok. I will wait for Di. I don't mind waiting for some more time" she said.
"Oh! But your mother will get worried. Please come with me." Gaurav offered her his hand.

She seemed hesitant. Just then Lokesh stepped from behind the tree & jumped on the girl covering her mouth to prevent her from yelling. He picked her up as she started kicking & scratching his arms with her finger nails.

"Couldn't you wait for 2 mins? She would have come with me." Gaurav asked frustrated with the impatience of his companion & scared that someone would notice them.

"We don't have time. Her sister will be out any minute & we aren't prepared to take them both. Ow!... She has got vicious nails!" said Lokesh noticing the grown almost feral nails for such a small child "Doesn't your mother cut your nails?" he asked irritated that she had managed to draw blood with her scratches. The girl continued to kick even more forcefully now while Lokesh tried to hold both her hands.

"Now tie her hands before she draws more blood you moron" Lokesh said to Gaurav swearing viciously in pain.

Gaurav took out the rope they had bought & just as he was about to tie up the hands of the little girl, he heard someone approach.

"Let go of my sister" said a girl about 11 with the same features as the one they were holding. The resemblance was uncanny. Anyone looking at the two girls would be able to make out that they were sisters.

The elder girl must have finished her extra class & now she was advancing through the veranda. However instead of being scared or yelling for help the way you would expect a normal child to behave, she just seemed to be very angry. The little girl seeing her sister had stopped biting & scratching. She was now looking at her sister. It was as if the two girls were communicating but Gaurav did not understand how that was possible with the younger girl's mouth being gagged. He doubled his efforts to tie the hands & feet of the younger girl.

"If you come nearer, we will hurt your little sister" said Lokesh brandishing a knife "You don't want that do you? So, stay where you are & make no sound" He asked with a maniacal glint in his eyes.

"I am giving you one last chance. Let her go" said the elder child in a calm & clear voice as her eyes started glowing.

Lokesh rubbed his eyes as he could not believe what he was seeing. The elder girl was smiling now & her eyes were glowing a bright red. Lokesh's grip on the knife weakened & then as if pulled by an invisible force, the knife flew through the air & dropped at the other end of the veranda, far away from Lokesh. He was shocked & kept staring as if unable to believe his eyes. Finally, he managed to get some words out.

"Gaurav, leave her! We... we need to go. Something is not right" said Lokesh shaking with fear as he dropped the younger girl. "Her... her eyes... they are glowing" he blabbered as he shook Gaurav.

Gaurav who was busy with the ropes was irritated at having the girl dropped almost in his lap. He was prepared to hit the child should she attempt to run. However, the girl seemed to be in no hurry to run so he continued to tie her hands & did not look up. To Lokesh he said "I told you that you need to be sober for today you idiot. I think this little girl is in shock. Now use the chloroform on both of them before anyone else comes out. We can't take any more risks" he said turning to his partner.

What he saw shocked Gaurav & it was a sight he would remember for the rest of his life. His partner was suspended in mid-air & was being turned round & round like a ball while the elder girl was smiling with her eyes glowing a bright red. Lokesh's eyes were opened wide in terror & his mouth was frozen in a scream with no sound escaping out.

"Who...what are you? Please ... please let me go..." Gaurav started pleading with the elder girl as he started backing away from the veranda.

As he backtracked, Gaurav almost ran into the younger sister. When he looked at her, he noticed that her eyes too had started glowing a bright red. The ropes he had used to tie her up had disappeared. She was now standing before him pulling the gag from her mouth & smiling. Gaurav rubbed his eyes to check if he was hallucinating – something he had accused his partner of but no matter how many times he rubbed his eyes or pinched himself, nothing changed. The little girl was now moving towards him.

"You should have run when you had the chance" she said as Gaurav too was lifted in the air.

Chapter 1 – Veena

"I want mauve curtains Veena not the onion pink ones this guy seems hell bent on convincing me are the same color," said Charmie. I internally rolled my eyes as she continued "Do you remember the painting in my foyer? I want my curtains to match the flowers in the painting. Is that so difficult to ask? I mean isn't that why I hired you?" asked my client, Mrs. Charmie Poonawala giving me a meaningful look.

"I am sure we can get the right shade. Isn't that right Vishal?" I asked the owner of the shop we were sitting in with a pointed look.

"I am not sure he heard you" said Charmie as she stomped her feet & directly approached the store owner- Vishal Thakur.

Vishal, who had recently taken over the running of the shop from his father was eager to extend his client base. He looked quite amused by the dramatic reaction of Charmie. Charmie or Mrs. Charmie Poonawala was the new daughter in law of one of the most influential families in Pune & a client I had thanks to my college friend. Handling difficult clients is part of my job & going out of the way for prestigious clients like the young lady in the shop with me is what keeps me young (yeah you guessed it- I love sarcasm). Charmie however was proving to be more difficult than most of my other clients. Having studied in London & travelled extensively; she had eclectic tastes. What I needed her to understand was that we could not recreate London in Pune! Be that for the outdoor materials she was demanding or the heavy drapes she insisted on choosing. The material would simply gather substantial amounts of dust in her Pune bungalow & the heat would fade the material within months of installation. Not to mention the nonstop complaints or rather barbed taunts I would get to hear from the Senior Mrs. Poonawala – Charmie's MIL who had taken me aside early on in my meetings with the younger Poonawala couple & told me in very clear words that while she more than welcomed the changes that her new DIL wanted to make in the décor, there were things which could not be compromised on - like her mandir or the huge tapestry that had been acquired at an auction by Mrs. Lata Poonawala. Replacing her newly installed embroidered organza drapes with this heavy chenille would be sacrilegious. Plus, the organza drapes were exactly the color that Charmie wanted & quite lovely.

Seeing that I had no other alternative, I decided that I would exercise my least preferred option. I signaled Vishal to give me some time alone with my client. I picked up a sample of cloth which was similar to the one installed in their current home & approached Charmie. I had already gathered from her thoughts that the color scheme she was fixated on reminded her of one of the lovely holidays she had taken in London with her friends & somehow her mind was associating the physical elements of the Air BnB she had rented with the enjoyment she had while on vacation. That was also the time she had met her husband & fallen in love. These were not things that Charmie had shared with me mind you. These were just things which I was able to gleam from her superficial thoughts. That is one of the powers I possess. I can read the most intimate thoughts in people's minds if I put some effort into it. I can also read a bit of their past & alter their moods – for I am a Rakshasi.

My name is Veena Pardeshi and I come from a family of Rakshasas. I am also an interior designer by profession as you may have already guessed. I live in Pune with my father, my Nani & my annoying little sister. I love my city & my job but in this world that is moving forward with technology and innovation, I often find myself caught between two realms. I walk the fine line between human and something more, something magical for magic is as much a part of my being as my fair skin or my brown eyes. Even though the common belief is that the Rakshasa race which evokes images of ancient legends and creatures is a part of mythology, it is of course not true. Though my race, once renowned for their sorcery, has gradually faded into the shadows, there are a few Rakshasas left as far as I know. We live among the humans. Most of us no longer wield our magic as a force of nature, for the world around us has shifted. The needs of today no longer align with the power we possess, relegating our ancient talents to mere whispers of a bygone era. Our families which were once united by shared abilities no longer feel the need to broadcast their presence by congregating to specific areas. They have dispersed across the globe to protect our heritage from prying eyes.

Mating with humans had also led to the magic dwindling in most lines of the rakshasa families. Human folklore describes us as dark, terrifying looking evil beings - which we are definitely not. But this image has worked to our advantage. Who would think that I tall, fair, slim & doe eyed Veena is a Rakshasi? My sister is also similarly endowed physically. Though Rakshasas in general can manifest in other forms- an ability which both my sister & I possess, this is how we were born - not as terrifying looking monsters that books & stories seemed to indicate. It was actually presumed that both me & my sister would not have any magic – the 3rd generation of half breeds which gave my father temporary relief. Yet, in a curious twist of fate, my sister Varsha and I possess a reservoir of magic that defies explanation. Our powers surge with a strength that should have been diluted through generations, a rarity in a world where our kind is fading & a puzzle for my father. As per my Nani who is treasure trove of all the magical knowledge & the intricacies of the Rakshasi bloodline, our lineage that had intertwined with humanity for generations had given birth to something new.

My mother had been a potent & extremely powerful half-blood Rakshasi. Her abilities were awe-inspiring, a blend of sorcery and enchantment that shaped my earliest memories. Yet, that very power had been a double-edged sword for her. Her strength had drawn both admiration and fear. It was a fear that though she never shared had haunted her throughout her life or the part that I could remember. I believed it was this fear which had led to her untimely departure from this world, leaving me & Varsha with fragments of a legacy which we yearned to understand. My father, Baba as I lovingly called him while sharing our lineage, did not possess the magic that defined our kind. Though his love was unconditional & his concern genuine, he could never truly grasp our connection to the magical world. After Ma's death he had completely turned his back on magic as well as our Rakshasa legacy. Determined to bring us up as normal human girls, he had locked away every possible object & kept away every possible person who could even accidentally give us a glimpse of the world he had decided was not for us. The only exception to this was my Nani- my maternal grandmother.

For us girls, my Nani is a living bridge to the world that once was. She had moved in with us shortly after Ma's death. Her diminutive stature painted her as a harmless if slightly eccentric old lady. Yet when people realize that there is nothing little about her other than her stature, they make it a point to stay on her good side. And that is just the way she likes it. Every time I look into her eyes, I sense the ancient currents of magic that flow through her veins, a testament to a power that's both formidable and enigmatic. I am pretty sure that whatever haunted my mother is a secret whose keeper is my Nani. She knows the nuances of our lineage- mine & Varsha's. She is the only one who possesses the knowledge that could unravel the enigmas of our abilities. But Nani understands the weight of our abilities. There's a sadness in her gaze that's coupled with an unwavering resolve. She has witnessed the price paid for wielding magic, and the pain it can bring. And in her wisdom, she respects the wishes of my father – though not necessarily agreeing with them. Sometime I feel she is bidding her time, waiting for a sign but maybe it is just my wishful thinking.

While Baba's resolve to shield us from the dangers that magic can bring- is born of pain, Nani has chosen a path born of love. While never overtly encouraging us to wield magic, Nani wishes for us to embrace our Rakshasa legacy. Her inner turmoil- wanting her granddaughters to know the essence of their being while at the same time wanting to protect them from the shadows that consumed my mother is often a cause of strife in our family. Yet, even as I respect my father's wishes and put up with Nani's silence, the hunger for understanding often gnaws at me.

I've caught glimpses of Nani's spellbooks, of ancient symbols that resonate with a primal part of me. I've seen the way my sister's eyes light up with curiosity, and I know that the thirst for knowledge is shared between us.

My world teeters on the edge of two realms— the shimmering echoes of our ancient lineage & the mundane reality of the present. Unknown to me though the delicate balance between these two reals has already been tilted & my choices will decide not only my destiny but also of those of my loved ones. For now, however my mundane reality is beckoning me in the form of a 25-year-old hell cat who if not handled right will walk out on her 2-inch heels costing me my hard-earned reputation.

"Charmie, I know you had your heart set on the mauve chenille drapes" I began "& I can get them for you. But have a look at this fabric. This will go much better with the furniture & the bedlinen you have planned."

As I spoke, I slowly implanted images of the existing flowing organza curtains in Charmie's mind along with a feeling of happiness & grandeur similar to what she was seeking. Normally, these things are against my principles. As has been instilled in me – I avoid using magic. I do not invade the minds of people in general & I have my own code of morals & ethics. However, when they are broadcasting their thoughts as openly as Charmie seemed to be there was no reason for me to not pick a few random ones amongst them & use them to my advantage. For me this was almost as unnatural to ignore them as it would have been had they been directly spoken to me.

"Actually" said Charmie touching the fabric sample I had picked up "I think we should leave the curtains as they are. Do you know my MIL picked them specifically for me & had them installed before our marriage & I really do like those curtains." She smiled.

One disaster avoided. I gave her a wide smile in return

"Sure, we can do that"

Just then my cell phone started vibrating.

"Give me one minute Charmie. It's my father & if I don't answer he will panic" I said rolling my eyes. "I will be right back. In the meanwhile, you can check the other brochures for the cushion fabrics."

I indicated Vishal to join us again with the said brochures & stepped outside to take the call.

"You do remember that you have dinner tonight right Veena?" My father had called just to remind me of my dinner plans with a prospective groom. I was reluctant to meet guys in an arranged marriage set up but it was something of an agenda of my Baba & my Nani to get me married before 28. So now this was my routine – meet one guy every alternate week. I had put my foot down saying I would agree to a second meeting only if we found anything in common. Till date no guy had made it to a second meeting. Maybe I was being a but picky... but the truth was I did not want to marry. These meetings were just to keep my family happy. Today I was meeting the fifth guy & this time too I had been unable to put my foot down & say no.

"Baba, I am coming home for lunch. Have you forgotten? Can we talk then please? I am with a client right now."

"Why are you disturbing her in the middle of a work day?" I could hear my Nani in the background.

"Veena beta. I am having your favorite chole bhature made." Yelled Nani.

"Give me another hour Nani. We are just finishing up here. See you soon Baba"

I ended my phone call & was just about to enter the shop again when I heard a couple of guys cat calling & whistling

"Hey how about a movie with me beautiful?" asked one.

Out of the corner of my eyes, I noticed it was 4 guys on 2 bikes who seemed to be ogling at me. I altered my facial features such that my nose elongated; my lips thickened & my chin jutted out with a nice mole & 3 hair sticking out at the bottom. Then I thickened my eyebrows & turned around to face the men with a smile exposing my large molars – also altered.

"Sure, boys I am ready! Which movie did you have in mind? "

The 4 men were so horrified with my appearance that they lost control of their bikes & crashed into the nearby tree. Thankfully as both the bikes were below cruising speed probably no one was hurt. As I started approaching them to check for injuries, they hurriedly started yelling

"Oh not you Behen (sister) we were not talking to you. We were talking to someone else."

Then all 4 got on their bikes & took off at 180 kms/hr. I burst out laughing. As I watched their bikes disappear around the corner, I noticed someone had parked behind me. I quickly changed my appearance again & turned around. The young man who had parked behind me was looking at me – his green eyes full of concern.

"Are you all-right? Were those guys bothering you?... I heard them"

Mr. Green eyes was quite handsome & I could see that he was also quite concerned. His eyes locked with mine & I could feel myself blush (something I very rarely do)

"I think they mistook me for someone else. I am ok but thanks for asking. I am Veena. Veena Pardeshi."

I extended my hand but he had folded his in namaste. Then he extended his hand while I folded mine, we both laughed at the exchange & as our fingers brushed when we finally did manage to shake hands, I felt a mild electric pulse race through my arm. I think he must have felt it too because we sort of jerked our hands away. Just as he was about to speak, I heard Vishal calling me.

"Veena can you please come in here?"

I said a hurried goodbye to Mr. Green eyes went inside without really getting his name but I had a nervous client to handle & I am a firm believer in fate. If we were to meet again then we would.

Chapter 2 – Disaster strikes

"Namaste, I am Veena Pardeshi. I am 26 years old & have my own interior designer firm. I am pretty head-strong, I like fast food & my favorite is paani-puri. And yeah, I am a Rakshasi!" Is that what I am supposed to say as my introduction to this new fellow you are asking me to meet Baba? What do you think would be his response when I tell him that I am a Rakshasi? Will he laugh or just run away or call the police?" I was asking my father post a delicious lunch. Trying to gauge his reaction.

"Why do you have to tell him that Veena? Why bring up the same topic every time?" asked Baba his forehead wrinkled in distaste

"Really Baba? Because it is a part of who I am. Am I supposed to hide it from the guy I am supposed to spend the rest of my life with?" I asked

"It's like you don't even want to give him a chance."

"Because I don't Baba. I am meeting him only for the sake of you guys." I said irritated.

"Just look at it as a free dinner di waise bhi ghar mein aaj raat ko bhindi ki sabji hain" my sister Varsha gave her input making a face.

None of us liked Bhindi except for my Nani.

"Why will he pay for my dinner Varsha? I can pay for my own dinner."

"Isn't it the norm for the boy to pay when he asks out a girl?" asked my Nani

"And could you please leave out the part about having your own firm as well?"

This was my father again- completely ignoring what I had said.

"No Nani, paying for your date was in your time & why shouldn't I tell him I have my own firm? I am not ashamed of it."

I said addressing both of them.

"He may not want such an independent woman & definitely not one with magic right Suhas?"

Nani pointedly ignored my response to her question focusing instead on what she wanted to communicate to my father. I was just a means. As I already mentioned, my magic & my lack of practicing it was a subject of constant strife in our house. Nani while deferring to my father's wishes was not in 100% agreement with his stance of keeping us girls away from all sorts of magic believing that it was a part of our very DNA.

"I can't believe you guys. Which century are you living in?" I was beyond frustrated with this conversation.

"Ok. Forget what your Nani said beta. Pay for your dinner & also tell him about your business. After all we are all very proud of you for what you have done with it. If he can't handle that then too bad" Baba said smiling

"But please do not mention the magic" he continued almost pleadingly letting me know to what extent he was willing to bend.

"You don't need it & you don't even use it that often." He looked at my Nani the challenge evident in his tone. She just shook her head & walked out of the room.

"Be sure to give him your business card as well" chimed in Varsha. "You never know where the next client comes from."

"Whatever! But please keep the Rakshasi bit to yourself Veena. Don't expose us" my father reiterated again & I nodded.

As I was talking, I was also packing all my materials & my laptop in my tote bag as I was already running late for my appointment with my new client.

"Ok Baba. I won't do that. But I am splitting the bill as I don't want any obligation from him." I replied

"Obligation kaisa di- he is getting to have his dinner with a beautiful girl. In my opinion he should be paying you just for your company" – Varsha was my true supporter, loyal to the core.

"Hide... hide who you are! All of you! No one here has one tenth of the spirit my daughter did"

Nani was mumbling to herself while getting ready for her afternoon siesta. Baba pretended to ignore her & smiled at me giving me a thumbs up.

"Now let me leave else Mrs. Sharma will cancel my contract even before meeting me." I said as I exited the house.

The rest of the day passed by quicker than I had imagined. Mrs. Sharma had taken me to her under construction apartment & elaborated on the ideas she had for the space. I had promised to get back to her with some design ideas. Then I had rushed to the designated restaurant 'Glocal Junction' to meet Mr. Sarthak Khare. The restaurant Sarthak had chosen was in the older part of the city and was expensive. It was the in-house restaurant of a 5-star hotel. Obviously, he wanted to demonstrate his wealth but the restaurant was known for its delicious cuisine so I wasn't complaining. Interestingly the place had a tragic history associated with it which probably was not known to Mr. Khare. Apparently 2 decades earlier the place was a bed & breakfast owned by a couple- the Gadre's. A fire had broken out in lodging in the middle of the night & while most of the people had managed to get out with the aid of the owners, a few had perished along with the owners themselves – the Gadre's. The story went that the Gadre's had no children & had started the lodging as a means to have more of a social life since they were lonely with no relatives in the city. The couple were also spiritual healers & many people who came for lodging also sought cures for ailments - physical but mainly mental which were a taboo to be discussed in those days. The couple stayed in a cottage at the back of the land parcel while the lodging quarters were built at the front. After their death the land had been passed to a distant cousin who had promptly sold it for the current hotel to be built. But, even after the land was sold & the hotel built, the small cottage at the back of the property was left untouched by the new owners. People claimed that it was because the cottage was haunted while some others said it was to maintain the history of the land. There were haunted tours conducted in the cottage over the weekends by the hotel itself & I was inclined to believe that the air of mystery added to the business of the hotel. After all there were quite a few people these days who were willing to pay extra to sleep in a haunted hotel. Some guests had claimed to her the sounds of the harmonium late in the night which was what Mrs. Gadre had taught the neighboring ladies in another attempt to socialize. I was pretty sure these were all rumors since I could not immediately detect anything unusual about the place. Nevertheless, it was a beautiful property & the haunted cottage could be seen at the far end of the lawns surrounding the hotel.

Sarthak arrived a few minutes late in his Mercedes. He was quite nice looking with a pleasant face & a fair if pasty complexion. After introductions, we walked inside & were taken to our table which Sarthak had reserved in advance. The restaurant ambiance was quite relaxed & the aromas wafting around made me realize that I had just had a cup of coffee after my lunch. My stomach growled in appreciation. As soon as the menu cards were handed, I placed my order for a Paneer shashlik with herbed rice without really reading through the menu. I had been to this place before & I knew considering the crowd that the food would take time to arrive. Sarthak seemed quite surprised at my hurry to place the order but then followed suit with his order for a paneer butter masala with garlic naan. (Garlic naan on a first date...? This guy definitely did not understand the subtleties of etiquette)

Once the orders were placed & the waiter had left the table, it was time to indulge in small talk. How I hated these! Just then, I heard tinkling female laughter followed by jaunty greeting "I will take my usual table". I turned around to see a plump broad chested man with a slight paunch being seated in a corner booth but what caught my attention was the woman by his side. She was dressed to the T for a casual dinner at a restaurant- like someone had forgotten to give her the dress code for the place. She seemed a bit conscious & kept looking around the restaurant. As they passed our table, our eyes met. Suddenly it felt like the restaurant had gone silent, like I had suddenly developed tunnel vision where I stood at one end of the tunnel & she stood at the other end. I forced my eyes away from her but I could see the surprise I felt reflected on her face as well. She was definitely magic & someone to be avoided. I tried to ignore the feeling & focused on my dinner companion.

Sarthak was in the construction business & worked with his dad. He started with small talk about the weather in Pune & then asked me if I liked sports. The minute I nodded; he launched in to a long tale of his favorite sport – cricket. He was apparently the captain of his club's team- which meant that the pasty complexion was not from lack of sunlight. I was bored in less than 2 mins but pretended to be paying attention while glancing at our surroundings. Two tables away from us was a tall guy with wavy dark hair & twinkling green eyes having coffee by himself. As I looked closer, I realized it was the same guy I had met outside of Vishal's shop. Talk about fate! Mr. Green eyes was speaking on the phone in hushed tones (probably to his girlfriend because let's face it a guy like him was bound to have one, right?) while stirring his coffee. Suddenly as if realizing I was observing him, he looked up & our eyes met. I smiled at him. On closer inspection, I noticed he had nice muscles & was sporting a stubble which somehow added to his appeal. In spite of being alone on the table he seemed to be at ease in the restaurant & not in a hurry to finish his coffee. He gave me a lopsided smile acknowledging that he too recognized me from our earlier meeting. I could feel a blush creeping on my cheeks & looked away before I embarrassed myself & glanced at the next table.

At the next table, the mismatched couple with the middle-aged man & the overly made-up willowy girl were seated. She was displaying her ample cleavage while having a conversation which was interrupted with the girl pouting at the camera to take her selfies. The guy was trying hard to draw her into a conversation & away from the camera. Try as I might I couldn't force my gaze away from their table. There was a sense of unease surrounding the table which was growing by the minute. Just then the waiter approached their table.

"Are you ready to place the order sir?"

"Whatever Nemina wants" answered the man.

"Can you get me one glass of your finest wine? And your vegan pizza please."

Announced Nemina after thoroughly analyzing the menu card on the table. The guy was a regular but it was definitely the girl's first time here I deduced.

"And for you sir?" asked the waiter again

"I will have a whisky on the rocks & the butter chicken with tandoori nan. And make it quick." Said the man as he typed out a quick text.

"Certainly sir," said the waiter.

I found myself to be really interested in this odd couple at the table. The restaurant seemed to be a family place & these 2 were anything but. The man pulled out a gift-wrapped box & handed it to the girl.

"Congratulations Nemina. You certainly deserve it." He said as he pecked her cheek exuberantly.

"Oh! That is so sweet of you. Can I open it?"

Nemina opened the box to reveal a thin white gold chain with a delicate diamond pendant. The man immediately put it on her slender neck. I was busy observing them when Sarthak interrupted my thoughts with a question.

"So are you following the IPL matches". Since I had no interest nor liking for cricket, I decided to be honest with him

"Actually, I don't watch cricket much".

"Oh, is that so? I think once you start watching you will quite enjoy it. I mean I know most women find cricket pretty boring but I figure you will like it."

I didn't understand whether he was insulting my whole gender or just praising me but I decided to give him the benefit of the doubt.

"I have passes to the next IPL match" he continued excitedly not registering my lack of enthusiasm.

This was officially getting a little out of hand. I had no intention of meeting Sarthak again – match or no match & I couldn't feign interest in cricket much longer. I was about to tell him this when danger alarms started sounding in my head & I felt a compulsive need to glance at the table where the middle-aged guy was seated. A red mist had started enveloping the table. As I looked around trying to gauge the reactions of the other people, I realized that there was no change in anyone else's demeanor. This meant that the mist was apparently visible only to me... or was it? The girl, Nemina (if I am not mistaken) looked panicked & her eyes were the size of saucers as she was desperately glancing around for help. The man on the other hand seemed oblivious to the mist.

I needed to get close to that table. I asked Sarthak to excuse me & got up presumably to go to the rest room but taking a route which took me past the table which was now completely enveloped in the mist which had become a dark pulsing red. Suddenly, the guy started foaming at the mouth & Nemina started screaming

"Oh my god! Mr. Khanna? Are you ok? Mehul?"

Chapter 3 – Mr. Green eyes

The guy at the table had collapsed & as I watched his body collapse, I saw the red mist around the table dissipating. I realized now that besides me there was definitely one other person who could see it – Nemina. But no one else seemed to be reacting to it – though they were reacting to the guy who had apparently collapsed at his table. Just as I was about to reach the table, Mr. Green eyes stepped forward taking charge. He checked the pulse of the guy & called out "Is there a doctor in the restaurant?" A lady from a nearby table immediately stepped forward. I waited while she took his pulse & confirmed that "Mehul" was dead. At her announcement chaos broke out in the restaurant.

People were pointing to the collapsed man & almost everyone had stopped eating. By this time the hotel manager had also reached the table. The foam at the mouth seemed to indicate that some kind of poison might have been used. Mr. green eyes spoke to the manager & subsequently the restaurant staff was dispatched to ensure that the panic did not spread. The customers were politely asked to continue to be seated at their tables & informed that due to the unforeseen incident, they would not be able to continue service. We were all informed that we would have to wait till the police got to the scene. Almost all the people started to complain stating that they needed to leave. However, the staff was firm. In a short while a young man wearing a name badge declaring his name to be inspector Aniket Jadhav entered with his team. I was quite surprised to see that the police had arrived at the scene within minutes while the nearest police station was at least 30 mins away but I kept that observation to myself.

The moment the police entered, Nemina started fidgeting in her seat. She mentioned that her brother was alone at home & that she needed to leave early.

"You see we...umm I don't really know him & it is getting late" I heard her say to the inspector.

I couldn't believe the nerve of this girl – leaving her dead companion who in all probability was paying not just for her meal but also her glittering jewels. Meanwhile the police instructed everyone to return to their tables & announced that we could leave as soon as they had our details & had questioned us. They started their questioning with Miss big boobs – that is what I had decided to call Nemina. Yes, I have this penchant for naming people basis their most prominent characteristic- sue me! So, Miss big boobs was led to one of the meeting rooms by the inspector. The police men started making the rounds gathering the details of the other guests.

"How unfortunate that this had to happen on our first date. I hope the next one will be more romantic" Sarthak was saying.

I cringed internally. There was never going to be a next meeting if I had my way. I had never in my life had a more boring dinner than with Mr. Cricket. I got myself excused from my excruciatingly tedious present company under the pretext of giving my details to the police. As I was navigating my way towards through the assembled crowd, I saw an apparition rise up from beneath the table & stare at the body. When I looked closely, I realized that it was the ghost of the dead guy. I was so surprised that I uttered a startled "You!".

Unfortunately, several faces had turned in my direction after my startled reaction. I had to make an excuse of feeling giddy having seen a dead guy for the first time (the body had not yet been moved giving me a convenient excuse. While I was mortified for having to do this helpless female routine, it would have to do for now.) My hysteria obviously brought all the aunties in the restaurant & Sarthak to hover over me as I was seated at a separate table near the air conditioning unit. The aunties were asking Sarthak if I was ok. Sarthak was holding out a glass of water for me. Meanwhile Mr. Khanna's- Mehul's ghost having realized I was the only one who could see him was yelling at me "Why is no one able to see me? Am I dead? I know you can see me..."

I was getting an acute headache. Fortunately for me that was the moment that the inspector Jadhav let out Nemina & called me in for questioning.

"Maybe you should ask her questions after everyone else is done" said Sarthak following me into the meeting room.

The inspector looked to Mr. Green eyes as if asking him for permission & I was at once suspicious of the dynamics between the two.

"Hello, I am Vinay. Vinay Verma" said Mr. Green eyes introducing himself as he shook hands with Sarthak. "Like James Bond" I couldn't resist asking to which Vinay just gave me a mischievous smile "More than you realize Ms. Pardeshi"

"Do you two know each other?" asked Sarthak picking up on Vinay knowing my name.

"Oh, we just met today morning but would like to meet again" said Vinay with a smile. He was purposely being vague but since he was getting me out of having to give an explanation, I went along with it.

"Umm... Yes actually."

"So, you met this guy said Sarthak pointing to Vinay "in the morning & then me for dinner?" He seemed to be getting a little worked up. "Well, isn't that packing it a little too tightly? Two men in one day?"

Sarthak had assumed I had met Vinay for the same purpose I was meeting him & I saw no reason to correct him. Before I could answer however, inspector Jadhav interrupted us.

"We need to question Miss Pardeshi now." But instead of ushering me in, the inspector again looked to Vinay.

"If miss (Vinay looked at me questioningly to which I nodded) Pardeshi is not feeling up to it I am sure the police don't mind talking to the others first, right inspector?"

I was quite surprised to see that not only had Vinay remembered my name but he seemed to have some in with the police. But I wanted to stay out of the dining room. The people there were making me claustrophobic not to mention the annoying ghost whom I was pointedly ignoring.

"No. No that is not a problem. I am ok. I just needed some water" I said stepping into the meeting room.

"Sir, we need to question Miss Pardeshi now. Could you please step outside?" said Inspector Jadhav pointing to Sarthak who reluctantly left the room.

"So, what brings you here Miss Pardeshi? Do you often come to Glocal Junction for dining?" asked inspector Jadhav.

Just as I was about to answer Mr. Green eyes or Vinay as I now knew him slipped inside the meeting room from the back door & stood in the corner. Along with Vinay, Mehul's ghost had also followed me inside. He was now trying to sit in the chair kept in the corner of the room but being non-corporeal & new at the ghost thing, he kept going through the chair. I was finding it difficult to keep myself from laughing but I knew that if I did that, the police would suspect I had a PTSD & that would not bode well for me.

"I am not comfortable speaking in front of an audience" I said pointedly looking at Vinay while ignoring the ghost who was now standing behind the inspector & trying to read from his notebook.

Inspector Jadhav turned around to see who I was looking at & immediately got up to salute. I was now confused. Who exactly was this guy?

"Mr. Verma is a detective. A plain clothes detective," said the inspector.

"These people won't be able to solve my murder." said Mehul's ghost derisively & then asked "Are you really just going to ignore me"

I was itching to question the ghost but I knew I couldn't do that in front of other people. I would have to wait. Mehul having realized that I couldn't or wouldn't speak to him shrugged his shoulders & wandered out of the meeting room.

"Thank you for joining in Sir." said the inspector.

"So, I just saw Nemina leaving" said Vinay "I hope you got all the details from her. I was going to join you here but some people out there were panicking so I got a bit late. I was surprised you let her go this fast..." Vinay looked to Inspector Jadhav questioningly. Aniket on his part was looking confused.

"What is wrong Aniket? I am talking about our prime suspect- the girl in red" said Vinay again referring to Nemina.

"Yes sir... I am trying to recollect"

"You ... you are trying to recollect?" asked Vinay with an incredulous look "I hope you at least got her contact number & her address?"

Aniket looked crestfallen at this assessment of the situation "Sorry Vinay...I mean Sir, I don't know what happened to me. It felt like whatever she was telling me was the truth"

"Let us continue in the adjoining room please" said Vinay as he indicated Aniket to join him in the smaller meeting room.

"Sorry Mr. Pardeshi. We won't be long" said Aniket with a flustered smile as he went into the adjoining room.

"So, what exactly happened Aniket?" asked Vinay. He was trying to keep his voice down but apparently these meeting rooms were not meant for having private conversations & in his anger Vinay had raised his voice. I couldn't help but eavesdrop as Aniket answered.

"She... she told me that her name is Nemina. She also said that she did not know the guy who was with her very well, that they had just met 2 days back & that he was a friend who had brought her here for dinner" Aniket answered slowly.

"What about her address & contact details? Did you get those?" asked Vinay patiently "We can call her in for questioning again"

"She said she is not from around here & that her SIM was borrowed from her friend"

"So basically, nothing Aniket! You haven't even taken her complete name leave aside her postal address or her contact number!"

Interrupted Vinay as he banged his something on the table in frustration " it's like there is no logic to your actions"

" You are right it was like I was under a spell" Aniket agreed

"Spell? Please don't start with your magic stuff Aniket. You know I don't believe in it. I think you are just exhausted after the late night you pulled. Don't attribute your tardiness to 'magic'"

Aniket wisely did not respond. But I wondered if Aniket's assessment of the situation was correct given my reaction to Nemina.

"We will get her statement later" said Vinay in a resigned tone. "The restaurant cameras have captured her & while a bit of an inconvenience it won't be very difficult to trace her" said Vinay in a resigned tone. "Let us continue with Miss Pardeshi's statement"

As Vinay & inspector Aniket came back into the meeting room, I tried to remember the question that the inspector had asked me before they left. "I was invited here by Mr. Khare for dinner" I said.

"You mean the gentleman with you – Mr. Sarthak Khare?" asked Vinay.

"Yes". I said tightly.

"Ok. And how do you know him?" asked Vinay curiously

"He is an acquaintance. In fact, this is the first time I am meeting him. My father had set up the meeting"

Vinay gave me a smile & I realized he had a dimple on his left cheek. This was a man who knew he was good-looking & must have been using that charm often on unsuspecting girls & ... damn if I wasn't prone to it either. All I wished was for us to be alone for some time so that I could get to know him better. I was surprised at my own reaction. I had never been this attracted to any guy before. Not even to Ravi my college boyfriend & my first crush.

"Oh so, was it a match-making meeting?" asked inspector Jadhav with a knowing smile

"Yes, it was." I felt the heat creep up my face. I was actually blushing!

"You were having dinner. Then what happened?" asked Vinay getting back to business at hand.

"Sarthak was talking about some IPL match & since I am completely not interested in cricket, I was bored & was looking at the people sitting at other tables" I said deciding that I would be brutally honest with the police. "Once I saw that there was something wrong with the man at the other table, I rushed to the table." I continued

"But that's where you are wrong" said Vinay thoughtfully "you see you rushed to the table before anyone else realized there was something wrong. Did you know that something was going to happen?" he asked looking directly at me

"Are you accusing me of something detective?" I asked angrily.

This guy clearly had a more astute sense of observation than I would have given him credit for. Going on the offensive was my only option.

"Why did you rush to the table? Did you know either the victim or his companion?" asked inspector Jadhav in a placating manner.

"No but I wanted to help if I could. I thought the gentleman at the table was going to get sick" I said trying to come up with a plausible explanation for my actions.

"How did you know that he was going to get sick?" asked Vinay not willing to let go

"I just... I had a feeling something bad was going to happen" I offered lamely "his companion also seemed to be panicking" I added

"Oh, so you had a 'feeling' did you? Sort of like a premonition? First him then you..." said Vinay sarcastically looking at Inspector Aniket.

"It happened, didn't it?" I confronted him

"Are you a trained medical professional?" asked Vinay changing tracks

"No, I am not a medical professional. I am an interior designer." I said confused by the question.

"So, what did you think you would be able to help with by rushing towards the victim?" he asked trying to make sense of the situation.

It was apparent that he felt like I was keeping something from him & I couldn't very well tell him about the red mist or the ghost without coming across as deranged.

"Well, isn't that natural?" I asked irritated with this line of questioning "When you see someone in distress shouldn't you want to help?"

Vinay & inspector Jadhav exchanged a look

"No actually, Miss Pardeshi. It is the opposite of natural. Most people when they see someone foaming at the mouth, get scared & prefer to walk away from the scene rather than towards it. Out of all the people in the restaurant you were the only one who walked towards the table" said inspector Aniket

"Well, I & him" I defiantly said pointing to Vinay

"Well yes." He said irritating me with that smile of his "But I am a police officer & you... well you are an interior designer"

"Are you insulting me? Or my profession?" I asked quite angry with Vinay now, dimple or no dimple.

"Relax Veena. I can call you that right? Veena" he went on without actually waiting for my response "your reaction was different than the reaction of most others."

"Well, what can I say? I like to help people. If that is a crime then you can arrest me." I decided on the spot that I wouldn't offer any more explanations.

Anything more & it would surely earn me a one-way ticket to a psychiatric ward.

"Ok! Maybe we got off on the wrong foot" admitted Vinay frustratedly running a hand through his hair. "Let me apologize" he said as he smiled at me again & gave me a wink.

Wait! are police officers allowed to flirt during an interrogation? I glanced at Jadhav but he was busy going through his notes.

"So what did you do after realizing that he was dead?" asked Vinay.

"Nothing. There was nothing I could do & you were blocking the path of everyone who tried to approach the table" I said.

"Point noted Veena. You need to chill. I think we are done for now. However, we will call you again if needed" he said nodding towards the inspector.

"And I would appreciate it if you kept my identity to yourself. It wouldn't do me well if everyone out there knew that I was a detective." He continued.

"Well, if you wanted it to be a secret why did you tell me either?" protocol be damned. This guy thought too much of himself.

"I took that call basis my experience & your reaction"

"Ya. My reaction. Because why would an interior designer rush towards a murder victim when she has no medical training & is too dumb to actually be the murderer. So dumb in fact that your secret is safe with me" I said angrily.

"You aren't going to let that go, are you?" asked Vinay.

I simply shook my head as I stepped out of the meeting room.

After questioning me the police went about taking the statement of the other people in the restaurant. Vinay had parked himself on the bar stool near the meeting room not interrupting the police in their procedure. As soon as I stepped out of the meeting room, I noticed that Mehul's ghost was trying to communicate with the other people in the restaurant. He was trying everything from blocking their path to yelling in their ears. But obviously they were unable to see or hear him though one child did get spooked. Finally getting angry he stormed towards me.

"I need to talk to you" he yelled in my face.

I knew I needed to make up some excuse to escape where I could be alone since Sarthak was stuck to my side asking me how I was doing & fussing over me in general. When the police gave us the all clear to leave, Sarthak asked me when would we be meeting next. I was trying to come up with an excuse which wouldn't be hurtful. Even though Sarthak had smirked when he assumed I had met 2 men on the same day including him, he was presumptuous enough to think that he would definitely be in the running for one more meeting. But before I could answer, Vinay interrupted us-

"So, we are meeting for drinks tomorrow, right? Around 7pm?" he asked

I understood what Vinay was doing by getting me out of having another meeting with Sarthak as well as guaranteeing himself a date with me...impressive! I went along with the charade.

"Umm... Yes actually."

Sarthak could gauge I seemed to be more interested in Vinay than him.

"Nice to meet you, Vinay." said Sarthak shaking Vinay's hand "I am sure Vinay here can drop you back since you seem to get along so well" he said exasperated "I have already paid the bill" he continued "so if you decide to join Vinay for drinks that will be one you"

I was officially livid with Sarthak's demeanor thankful that I had not taken by father's advice of taking a rickshaw just so that Sarthak could drop me back home. Mehul's ghost was observing the interactions amongst the 3 of us with amusement. He did not seem to be particularly surprised about his death & I wanted to know why.

"I think I won't drink tonight & I certainly don't need anyone to drop me back. In case you didn't notice I have my own Scooty & I plan to ride back on it on my own" I said glaring at Sarthak.

"Whatever suits you. Good night, Veena & it was nice meeting you." Sarthak offered a wave & left.

That left me with Vinay. He was still smiling at me & getting a little irritated I asked him "Don't you have a job to do?"

"My team is on it & they are very efficient. It is actually quite late so let me accompany you back home." before I could respond he continued "I know you have your scooty let me just follow you on my bike to ensure you reach home safely. The questioning took long & it is quite late. Your parents must be worried."

"My parents! What makes you think I live with my parents?"

"Don't you" asked Vinay confused at my reaction & I realized that he did not make that assumption to insult me.

"Yes, I do." I said adjusting my tone. "But they know I can take care of myself & I travel late many a times."

I explained quite sure that Baba would have assumed my dinner was going splendidly since I hadn't returned home.

"I would still like to accompany you just for my peace of mind. After all I am sure they would be expecting Sarthak to drop you." said Vinay.

I shrugged. "Ok! just let me get freshened up" I said.

I didn't understand why I was getting so irritated & flustered with Vinay. He was hot & I definitely wanted to spend time with him but I was probably irritated at myself for having that reaction to a man. As I pondered over this on my way to the washroom, I signaled for Mr. Khanna or rather his ghost to follow me.

Chapter 4 – Dark Musings

One more threat was successfully eliminated today. In all my years in my new life, this guy had come the closest to exposing me. I would have to be more careful going forward. The world was certainly changing. My plan was already in motion & I relished this first victory. I shut the door of my dressing room & as was my habit sat down in front of my dressing mirror.

I looked at the mirror & as usual my reflection brought a smile on my face. My hair was still thick, dark & lustrous inspiring men to write poetry. I observed with a detached interest my kohl lined eyes which could go from guileless to shrewd, my thick eyelashes which shielded my intents while drawing in my victims, my full lips which could offer the softest kiss & the wildest nibble, my straight nose which ended in a sharp jawline driving men to distraction, my high cheek bones which had inspired many men to rebel against their families, their morals. But all of my beauty was just my visible assets. My beauty waylaid men by giving them a false sense superiority which they so craved and a feeling of possession of a beautiful being - a trophy to be displayed; which I ensured they always got.

Then as was my habit born as much out of caution as pride, I went a bit closer to the mirror & touched my reflection. I started noticing the minute wrinkles that had started appearing near my kohl lined eyes, the laugh lines that threatened to turn my smile into a frown, the fat that threatened to puff out my cheeks & the most worrying of it all my dark hair which had started greying at the temples. Right now, make-up & hair dye was allowing me to maintain my crown but not for long... surgery wouldn't help either. That was never going to be an option for someone like me. I would need to feed & soon. This time I would need a full boost. No halfway measures would work. Lately I had noticed that I needed to feed more & more often & unless

I found something or more specifically someone, I would fade away faster & faster as time went by. Not long back I had assumed that it would be really difficult if not impossible to find a magical entity who would give me enough of a power boost to get rid of all these tell-tale signs of ageing once & for all. But fate had been kind.

I had found my victim & she was perfect. Today I had killed 2 birds with one stone – getting rid of the one who threatened me & finding myself a new magical meal.

Now my favorite part was about to begin. It was time to start the hunt...

Chapter 5 – Mr. Khanna

Before entering the loo, I finally acknowledged the ghost simply because I didn't want him to see me while I was doing my business.

"Yes Mr. Khanna, I can see you. Now can you please wait here while I pee & then we can talk."

"Finally! I knew you could see me" he said

"Again - Yes. I can see you! Now stand there while I go & pee. You can't come in there or else I won't listen to you" I said indicating to one corner of the washroom.

"But... but I know that I have died so how are you still able to see me? Even Nemina couldn't see me. I think only you can see me. Why is that?" he asked

"Because I am a Rakshasi Mr. Khanna. I have always been able to see & talk to ghosts. But if I started talking to you in the presence of others, they will think I have gone mad." I replied patiently "Is that what you want? Now stand aside & let me pee." I continued not letting him answer me.

"Ok! Ok! No need to get angry. Geez...women" said the ghost rolling his ethereal eyes

"It would do you well to remember that this woman is the only one who can see you right now. A little respect might be in order don't you think?" I asked my anger evident from my expression.

The ghost seemed to get the message & obediently went to the corner of the washroom as I entered the stall to pee. The magic I possessed enabled me to be able to talk to ghosts & the ability to read minds. I rarely if ever used the mind reading thing & I had been fortunate enough to not encounter many ghosts. So having a chat with one was a rarity for me.

When I was washing my hands, my curiosity got the better of me & I asked "Was that your girlfriend? Did you know she wanted to run away the moment she realized you were dead?"

"Nemina, you mean... she is no one" said Mehul.

"Really it didn't seem like she was no one. In fact, it looked like you guys were really close" I replied

"Look what do you want me to say? Look at me & look at her. Can't you guess who she was?" he asked

"Was she a hooker?" I asked horrified at his implication.

"No nothing so crass. She was my ...assistant. My personal assistant" he said with eyes full of lust.

"Yuck! Did you just give me that look? Shut your eyes right now" I demanded disgusted with this lecherous ghost.

"I would have shown you a good time had I still been alive you know" said Mr. Khanna's ghost "you are a beautiful girl."

"I am a Rakshasi & you are dead! I am also the only one who can see you right now. Are you sure you want to continue with this behavior? I can go back to ignoring you or...- I can banish you." I said sternly. It was better to set some ground rules.

Instead of the getting scared though, my warning seemed to have the opposite effect. "You know you remind me of a black widow. Do you know what a female black widow spider does Veena? She kills her mate" said the ghost with a dark lustful look

I just looked at him surprised by the vehemence on his face. If he had still been alive, I would have kicked him in the groin but since he was now beyond pain, I said "Banish it is. Bye Mehul" I raised my hands.

"No...no please don't do that. I am sorry for what I said" said the ghost with fear in his voice.

I can banish ghosts if I choose to but I don't know what happens to their souls when I do that which was why I was hesitating. There was also one more reason why I reigning in my temper - Mr. Khanna had not died of natural causes & I wanted to ensure that the murderer was brought to justice. This ghost however was testing my limits.

"Look, I know I haven't been a very good human being but I have a family & I love my children very much. At least let me ensure that whoever has killed me means no harm to my family." He sounded sincere & his family especially his children deserved protection, so I decided to give him a chance.

"I will help you but you will have to communicate with me only when we are alone. No bothering me in a crowd & no invading my privacy. Got it?"

"Yes Ma'am" said the ghost mock saluting.

"I am very tired right now. We will talk tomorrow." I told the ghost.

"But... but wait. There is something I need to tell you..." said Mehul's ghost.

"You have 30 seconds after that I will walk out from here"

"I think... I think that I have been killed with magic," said the ghost looking straight at me

I was flabbergasted – how could this guy know how he was killed? I decided to get to the root of the matter. "How do you know how you were killed?" I asked

"So, it's true then" he said with a sad smile suddenly looking older than his years.

"Do you know who killed you Mr. Khanna?" I asked with an urgency in my voice.

"I don't know who killed me but I can make a very good guess ...I just need to check something first" he said & then before I could ask him to stop, he disappeared in front of my eyes. I tried calling him back but figured that perhaps he needed some confirmation after which he would approach me himself. Since I did not know many magical beings in the city & most of the ghosts seemed to find their way to our house, I assumed that it would not be any different for Mr. Khanna. Perhaps I should have waited or actively engaged my magic to call back the ghost but I did neither. Had I known the consequences of my actions I might have reconsidered though I don't know if that would have changed the outcome...

When I exited the bathroom, I found Vinay speaking softly on the phone. He hung up on seeing me saying he would call back. My curiosity was spiked but I was waiting for him to explain the situation.

"So... shall we leave?" he asked

"Yes. Let's" I agreed.

"I can see that you have some questions. Let us get out of here & I will explain."

"Sure" I said.

We rode on our 2 wheelers with Vinay maintaining a comfortable distance between us. As we reached near my bungalow, we parked our bikes & Vinay walked over to me. In this close proximity, I could see his muscles bulging from his cotton t-shirt. He was too good looking to be just a cop so what was he doing working for the police? He should have been a model. Umm... what exactly was Vinay saying now?

"Are you listening Veena?"

OMG was I really drooling? Vinay gave an easy smile as if he could read my thoughts but decided to let me off the hook by continuing "I will begin by saying that the lesser you know the better it will be for you. Now with that caveat in place do you really want to know what I was doing at the restaurant?"

I knew I should not get involved – don't get me wrong I do not actively seek trouble but in this case, I had already made promise to a ghost & what better way to track a killer than to collaborate with the police? And no this had nothing to do with the attractiveness or the taut muscles of the lead officer. I nodded to Vinay.

"Mr. Mehul Khanna is... was suspected mafia. There have been a lot of suspicious deaths surrounding him. I was deputed to spy on him, if possible, get a job in his firm & report back on his activities."

"You mean the potbellied, mild mannered lecherous man with thinning hair was godfather?" I asked surprised at Vinay's revelation.

"Appearances are always deceptive" said Vinay ruefully.

"In the past 5 years or so a number of people associated with Mr. Khanna have gone missing mysteriously or have suffered strokes when they wanted to volunteer any information to the police. We have tried to find out what exactly is the nature of his business but haven't gotten satisfactory answers. On the face of it he was running a law firm but the business he gets does not justify amount of money he is making. He has also been sued by the legal heirs of some of his clients for fraud," explained Vinay

"What sort of a lawyer was he?" I asked curiosity getting the better of me.

"He was a property lawyer to whom a lot of his clients bequeathed their assets to & then mysteriously disappeared or died" Vinay informed me "We suspect that he is running illegal gambling joints & has a stake in multiple drug rings but all of it is conjecture at this point."

"But then why haven't the police ever arrested him then?" I asked incredulously for surely a man like this should not be roaming around freely.

"Because at the time of the deaths or disappearances, Mehul was never even in the same city," said Vinay.

"The whole operation sounds sleazy. I wonder why would people continue to go to him for legal advice?" I said thinking aloud.

"I think it's because he has kept his business moving. He has moved to Pune only recently but before this he had offices in Nashik & before that in Satara. Also, he managed to keep the claims of the heirs from getting out & apparently, he was very good at his job," said Vinay.

"So do the police suspect that he had his clients murdered" I asked in horror. This situation seemed to be getting more & more bizarre. The ghost I had spoken to did not seem to be as innocent in hindsight as I had initially thought.

“Not all of his clients for sure. I believe at least one of his clients or their heirs had him killed as revenge. That is what we need to find out.” Vinay voiced out his suspicions.

While I found the information fascinating, I doubted that a human any human for that matter was responsible for the death I witnessed. The ghost also seemed to agree. We were definitely dealing with something paranormal here. Something that Vinay & his colleagues would never be able to understand. I needed to check on this with my Nani.

As I opened the gate to park my Scooty I noticed the curtain flutter on the ground floor of the bungalow next door. I was sure this was my nosy neighbor Mrs. Joshi who was spying on my comings & goings to report back to the whole society. No doubt tomorrow she would be asking my father innocently about the green-eyed man who had come to drop me home & if my ‘rishta’ had been fixed. I waved good bye to Vinay & asked him to proceed indicating the open curtain with my eyes. He seemed to get the message & left. Varsha was waiting for me when I reached home.

“Is Sarthak going to be my new Jijaji?” she asked teasingly.

“Sarthak... Who is that?” I asked as I was brushing my teeth my mind busy with what Vinay had narrated regarding the business of Mr. Khanna, the possibility of there being another paranormal in my town & the information provided by the ghost himself

“Sarthak – Sarthak Khare. The guy you just had dinner with” said Varsha shaking my shoulder. “Where are you Di? Did something happen?” she asked narrowing her eyes.

My sister is able to judge my moods faster than anyone else & there was no sense in keeping things from her. I wanted Varsha’s thoughts on what happened at the hotel & aside from my Nani she was the only one I could confide in about the paranormal bit. So, I narrated my entire evening to Varsha.

"Do you think the Gadre ghosts had anything to do with the murder" she asked suddenly.

The haunted cottage on the property & the story of its owners was known to all in the city though we had never had the opportunity to take the tour. I yawned. That thought had not even entered my mind. But I dismissed the possibility as soon as I had thought of it.

"If I could see the ghost of the dead man Varsha surely, I would have been able to see 2 other ghosts who supposedly haunt the place. Besides what motive could they have had?" I asked stifling another yawn. I was going to be asleep on my feet if we continued this conversation.

"Maybe they are bored of each other & just wanted company" replied my sister cheekily.

"No. It was something else. Something I haven't experienced before." I said remembering the alarm bells that had gone off in my head just before Mr. Khanna died.

"Looks like you have had an eventful night Di" said Varsha as I yawned again. "I will let you sleep for now but tomorrow I want all details of detective Vinay & his green eyes she said winking at me.

"There is nothing to tell" I said a little irritably.

"Oh, is it then why is he calling you right now?" said Varsha snatching my mobile from the bed.

"Give me my mobile Varsha" I said trying to snatch the phone from her as she jumped on the other side of the bed sidestepping me.

Since I was too tired to play tag with my sister I said "Ok. I will tell you all about him tomorrow. Now hand me my phone" On hearing this, Varsha tossed me the phone gave me a thumbs-up & flounced to her own room humming 'koi mil gaya' as I rolled my eyes.

What could Vinay possibly want this late in the night? I wondered. Hadn't we just said good bye like half an hour back? I answered the phone without sounding too excited (which I obviously was)

"You actually dropped one of your earrings on the road near the restaurant Veena. I was going to return it when I dropped you but I think you wanted me to leave." said Vinay.

I instinctively reached for my ear lobes & noticed that indeed one of my earrings was missing. These were my favorite pair of rings with pearls.

"It's not that I wanted you to leave. Actually, our neighbor is very nosy & I didn't want to give her anything to talk about"

"And you thought if I stayed, she definitely would have something to talk about?" asked Vinay in a teasing tone.

"Thank you so much for finding my earrings" I said sidestepping his question. "Should I come down now to collect them?"

"No, I have actually reached home. It was too late so I thought I could come down to your office & hand them over if that is ok with you?" he asked.

"Sure. Call me before you drop in. I have to go browsing for some picture frames tomorrow but I will wait for you" I responded sleepily

"Nice. May be next time I will come to browse with you. My apartment can use some décor."

Vinay was saying text book cheesy stuff but somehow coming from him it sounded genuine. He was the first guy I had connected with before we even spoke. He was not just good looking but there seemed to be a genuine warmth to him & his eyes seemed to actually speak to me. I did not want to be a girly girl but with Vinay that is who I felt like.

"Are you there?" I realized Vinay had asked me something & I was so lost in thought that I hadn't answered.

"Yes 10.30 am would be fine."

"It's a date then. Coffee at your office. Goodnight Veena" he said.

"Goodnight Vinay." I turned around to find Varsha breathing down my neck. "Goodnight Vinay" she said batting her eyelashes, imitating me apparently. When had she come back?

"Go to bed Varshu. I am really tired. Tomorrow morning, I will tell you about Vinay. That's a promise."

"Goodnight Di" said Varsha pecking me on the cheek.

Chapter 6 – Family matters

The next morning, as I went to pick up the newspaper from the drop box, I saw Mrs. Joshi sitting in the veranda of her bungalow.

"Good morning, Veena. Who had come to drop you last night dear? Was it one of the boys your father set you up with?" she asked "Actually, I think my nephew will be a perfect match for you- that is if you haven't found anyone yet" she continued without giving me a chance to answer.

"Good morning, Joshi aunty. They guy who had come to drop me is a friend. I am actually not that keen to get married right now. I just go meet boys to keep my father happy" I replied with a smirk.

Mrs. Joshi did not know how to react

"But why don't you want to get married? Are you involved with anyone?"

God! she could be so nosy. I was still trying to be civil.

"No. nothing like that aunty. I just haven't found the right person besides I think I am too young to get married"

She squinted at me through her glasses

"Your entire generation is the same. Women in our generation were a lot more practical but who listens these days? My nephew also doesn't want to get married. Wants to fall in love! Well, you have a good head on your shoulders & you will know when the right guy does come along. Run along now. Suhas would be wanting his paper"

I waved to Mrs. Joshi & started skimming through the news as I walked inside. In a corner there was a small news article about the murder at the restaurant. There was also a line mentioning that Mr. Khanna was survived by his wife, Mrs. Pinky Khanna & two kids aged 4 & 17. So, the ghost really was telling the truth with regards to his family. Next to the news article was an announcement for the Shok-Sabha to be held over the weekend at the bungalow of Mr. Khanna with the timings & the address. This was the first time probably that the Shak-

Sabha date was being announced on the same day as the murder. Was the family already prepared for his death? Playing on a hunch I decided I would go to the memorial to get more information about my ghost so that I could help him out.

Handing the paper to my father, I took a hurried shower & donned my favorite pair of jeans with an oversize tee. Then I joined my family at the breakfast table. Figuring that it was better to lay out everything that had happened the previous evening instead of waiting for my father to quiz me, I told Nani & Baba all that had happened at the hotel in an abridged version. I also told them about the red mist I saw & the girl that Mr. Khanna was dining with. "So, the ghost is probably waiting for me at our gate" I concluded.

"You are saying that the guy who died was a criminal who was probably with a hooker?" asked my father alarmed.

"The quality of people coming to Glocal junction has certainly gone down" clucked my Nani.

"Certainly. When we had gone there it was all families," said Baba not understanding the sarcasm in Nani's statement. According to her my father was a prude.

"That is what is bothering you? Seriously? You are unbelievable!" I said looking at Varsha as both of us rolled our eyes.

"If I had known that these kinds of people visit that place, I would never have recommended it to Sarthak" continued Baba as though I hadn't spoken.

"You had recommended that restaurant to Sarthak? I thought you didn't know where I would be dining." I asked accusingly

"Well, he doesn't step out much & asked me for advice what was I supposed to do?" said Baba dismissively.

"How about let me decide then?" I said irritated.

"Oh, you would probably have taken him to a coffee shop like the last 3 guys then had a mocha & left in 20 mins. Your father wanted you to give this guy a chance" said Nani suddenly switching sides as she smiled slyly "Though why him I don't understand. It's not like he is a Rakshas" she continued with a pointed look directed at my father.

I had full faith that these 2 would get into the Rakshasa debate again & decided to deflect before the conversation veered.

"Baba & Nani will you please stop interfering so much in my life. Why can't you guys check up on Varsha more often? Her college ends at 3.30pm but she never comes home before 5. Why not ask her what she does in between?" I asked throwing Varsha under the bus to maintain the peace.

"Hey what did I ever do to you?" asked Varsha pulling on my shoulder for me to look at her.

"I know what she does," said Nani. "She is hanging out with that Harry- who is also not a Rakshas" Trust Nani to not let go of her point.

"You mean Harish?" my father asked. "The guy who works in IT & comes & goes at odd hours?"

"Yes. I hang out with Harry. I like him & if you have a problem with that then it's too bad!" interrupted Varsha as she glared at Baba & Nani.

I silently mouthed "Sorry" but she ignored me.

"Harish is a good boy but he is more fond of music than studies," said Baba.

"So what? he can have a great career ahead of him if he is good. Did you know I was also in a rock band in college," said Nani.

Out of all the grandparents I had known in my lifetime my Nani definitely took the cake for being the coolest. She adhered to no social norms & had often regaled us with hilarious & amusing stories of her young age.

"Yes, Nani we all know about the 'Jungli Chudails'" Varsha & I yelled out together as we burst out laughing.

"Well, anything is better than dining with criminals" said my father with a frown the conversation once again coming back to me.

"Suspected criminal Baba. They have not found anything concrete on him that is why Vinay was trailing him. And may be seeing as how your choice was so horrible, you will let me choose a restaurant or a coffee house the next time around" I took a jab

"But there may not be a next time" said Varsha giving me a sly look "Did you know that Vinay dropped Di back home. Not Sarthak - Vinay!" Varsha was getting me back for leaking her secret to our father. Oooo I could strangle her!

"And this Vinay is a cop?" Asked Nani- her full attention on me.

"A plainclothes detective" said Varsha enjoying the conversation now that it had moved once again to me.

"He was just being polite Nani & aren't you getting late for college Varshu?" I asked annoyed.

"He is also very handsome" continued Varsha as if I hadn't spoken.

"How on earth do you know that?" I asked frowning.

"Oh, I saw his DP when he called you last night" shrugged Varsha as if it was the most natural thing to do.

"So Sarthak really didn't come to drop you?" Baba still seemed to be stuck on Sarthak.

"No Baba. I told you I was bored to death talking to Sarthak. We said good bye at the restaurant itself." I explained for though my patience was now wearing thin,

"But how can you ask a strange man to accompany you back home so late at night?" asked Baba.

"Suhas, he is a police detective," said Nani. "Isn't that what she just said?"

"Did he show you his badge" asked Baba "These days anyone can pretend to be a police officer."

"Sure & then hire people to play his team & then fake a murder to impress a girl why not? That is the world we live in now!" I rolled my eyes again

"Don't be a smartass Veena" Nani admonished "Harassing your father is my domain" she chuckled.

"Yes. He showed me his badge Baba," I replied in resignation. "All the policemen who were conducting the investigation seemed to defer to him. Besides have you forgotten that your daughter is a Rakshasi & can take care of herself?" I asked exasperated.

"Oh, he wants to forget that every moment of every day dear" said Nani immediately.

"Not now Nani" I said tired of this conversation.

"Both our girls can take care of themselves" said Nani addressing her words to Baba this time.

"Yes, but we don't want to invite trouble. I don't want any policeman looking into too many details of our family" replied Baba with a pronounced frown

"Vinay won't do that" I replied indignantly.

"But if he does what exactly will he find Baba?" asked Varsha. "You keep mentioning such vague things but never tell us why is it such a bad thing for any of us to be a person of interest with the police or to get too much recognition"

"There are things in our past which cannot be easily explained if someone decides to investigate" said Nani without going into the details.

She exchanged a weighted look with my father. I knew this had something to do with Ma's death. I was old enough to remember the sense of dread I had felt after her passing but Varsha had been too young to recall anything.

"Do you girls remember what happened when you were in school?" Asked Baba deciding to confide details regarding another incident which was still fresh in Varsha's mind as well as my own. I remembered this incident as if it had happened yesterday. It had been a few years after Ma's death. Baba was doing his best to be a single parent but it was not easy. Nani had lived nearby but not with us then. The 2 thugs who had come to kidnap Varsha had got more than they bargained for. We never really understood how Baba & my Nani had managed to bury that incident.

"Those 2 men deserved what they got" continued Baba "but do you know how hard it was to convince the police & the school staff that 2 drug addicts had not only decided to confess & go to jail but were willing to turn witnesses for the prosecution?"

"You had really done a number on their brains Veena" said Nani with a chuckle.

"Well like Baba said they deserved it & I did not know how to use my powers back then"

"And now you do?" asked Nani with narrowed eyes. "You haven't learnt to wield your magic even now my child"

"And neither will she" said Baba with determination "she does not need magic"

"Really Suhas! who was going to save her at the school if not her magic?" challenged Nani.

"I am sure one of the teachers would have seen them & called for help" said Baba stubbornly.

"You keep telling yourself that Suhas. I am sure Swati would have wanted her daughters to embrace their legacy" pushed Nani.

"Not now! Please Naliniji. I beg of you" said my father folding his hands in supplication a pained look on his face. But this time my Nani ignored it. It was the first time I had seen her not leave her stance.

"You think you are protecting them but I know that they need their magic & I hope you realize that before it is too late," said Nani. "Do you really think that we are the only magical beings mingling among humans Varsha?" Nani asked looking at the 2 of us. Though the magic debate was an ongoing battle in our house for as long as I could remember, I couldn't remember my Nani warning my father the way she had today. I think the episode with the ghost had bothered her more than she was letting on.

"You mean there are others like us?" asked Varsha

"Of course, there are. We have been very careful to raise you in a protected environment but there have been times when other entities have tried to disturb our peace. They have tried to take our power. We have successfully managed to end those threats but that does not mean that there won't be more. It also means that we always should avoid detailed scrutiny by any government agency because magic cannot be explained" Nani clarified looking at me.

As I pondered over Nani's words, my heart seemed to drop a little. Why was it that I had to fall for a guy who not only didn't believe in magic but was the very definition of the people we needed to avoid?

"Cheer up di. May be Vinay will be an exception" whispered Varsha sensing my mood.

I gave her a small smile.

Chapter 7 – Parampara Designs

After finishing breakfast, as I was about to leave, my phone started ringing incessantly "Oh Veena, you have to help me" sobbed Charmie. In all the excitement of the previous evening I had forgotten to call my young client which I had been doing since the time the project had started. Charmie needed constant attention & validation from those around her. "Anil hates the frames I had chosen" I was pretty sure she was blowing things out of proportion but cajoling high strung people was part of my job.

"Did he tell you he hates them, Charmie?" I asked patiently

"No but every night when I show him the changes, I am making in our sitting room he tells me how nice everything is shaping up. Last night, he did not say a single word when I showed him the frames. Just told me he was tired & then went off to sleep. Then today morning he had already left before I woke up" And she was sobbing again.

I sympathized with Anil. While he had married his college sweetheart who was very pretty & indeed a sweet person, his lack of enthusiasm even at the teeny-tiniest of things could send her over the edge. Anil was the acting CEO of his father's company & his work kept him busy. While he had joined in a couple of meetings with Charmie, he had largely been absent in the others leaving the major decisions of the décor to his wife. I had patiently heard Charmie complain of his busy schedule & lack of time for her so many times that I had lost count. I had even joked with my staff that Anil should be paying me for marriage counselling considering the amount of time I was spending giving relationship advice. My guess was that rather than not liking the frames, Anil would have been too tired to comment on them. I calmed down my client saying that I would speak with Anil & get his opinion & change the said frames if he genuinely did not like them. I then sent a short message to Anil on WhatsApp asking him to call me through the day as time permitted. Then as an afterthought I added that Charmie was upset & that between us we could sort it out.

I was expecting Mr. Khanna's ghost to approach me as soon as I stepped out of the wards surrounding our house. But when I stepped outside, Mr. Khanna's ghost was nowhere to be found, leaving me with a sense of confusion. Why had he not returned? Had he found someone else who could help him? The few ghosts I had dealt with had all seemed impatient to get their last wishes completed so they could move on so why was he different? I felt a distinct sense of unease. The confusion of his absence was a reminder that the supernatural world was as vast and unpredictable as the human one. While I was adept at navigating the human world, the magical one still held its secrets guardedly from me. Unwilling to surrender them till I joined it. I thought back to the previous night. Mr. Khanna had mentioned he needed to check something but had never returned. One thing that I had not taken into account though was that Mehul had been killed by magic. So, was it possible that his killer could also see his ghost? Pondering would get me nowhere.

Since I was already running late thanks to Charmie's hysterics & figuring that I could tackle the ghost later in the day, I took off on my Scooty to my office. Parampara – Heritage designs was the fruit of many years of hard work. Fresh out of design school, I had at first interned with a few design firms but had slowly come to realize that most of them had reservations. When it came to design choices, they preferred to work with the tried & tested materials & tried & tested vendors. They were averse to risk as it would affect their reputations & in most of the cases managed to convince their clients that the tried & tested options were always the best. There were few who were willing to experiment in their own homes. But with the likes of Netflix exposing the Indian audiences to newer materials, better ways to utilize their space & assure them of the workability of these innovations, I figured I had found my niche. I started with designing small spaces for clients with a shoe string budget. The main objective in those first few projects was simple- the best & most optimal utilization of every sq ft of available space. Slowly & steadily my client base grew as did my reputation. While still considerably small than the other bigger firms, my company now boasted the repute of a boutique design firm. I had a trusted contractor with whom I had started out & my trusted suppliers. It was less than a year back that I had finally been able to purchase my own office though on loan & it meant the world to me.

When I reached the office, I found Vinay waiting with a bouquet of Lilies. He greeted me at the door.

"How did you know I love Lilies" I asked.

"I didn't but I love lilies & roses are cliché, orchids are well foul smelling. Lilies are so 'you'" He smiled & gave me the bouquet.

I blushed as I accepted the flowers unlocking the door of my office.

"This is a very artistic door" said Vinay as he admired my mauve door with gold filigree "I love your sense of style".

"How do you know that I designed this door? It could have been designed by my employers" I asked genuinely curious about his response.

Most of the guys I had met or interacted with earlier, seemed to think I worked at Parampara & someone else was in charge.

"I think you work for yourself" said Vinay thoughtfully "You are too talented & too independent to work for someone else"

I had indeed designed the said door & named my business - 'Parampara – heritage designs' after the emotions I wanted to generate in people after hearing it. I was quite proud of both.

"You are right" I said smiling "you see being an interior decorator my door is my first advertisement".

For Vinay to have not only noticed but appreciated my work made him aces in my book. That I was a business owner & a successful one at that, did not seem to overwhelm him. So far, I was liking everything about Vinay. His shirt, his cologne, his hair, his muscles, his manners, his dimple (OMG that dimple) his green eyes & his soft lips.

I sat down in my favorite lounge chair behind my desk. I had found the chair in an old furniture shop & had fallen in love with its carved design. I had gotten it painted & re-upholstered.

Meanwhile Vinay looked around the office. In my current setup my office was my home away from home. It was a calm oasis for me to work from. Most of the client meetings took place at the venue or the place they wanted to get decorated. However, in spite of many of my clients preferring to meet outside, I had put in a lot of effort to make my office feel as welcoming as possible.

The first thing I had done was to replace the standard sliding windows which covered one entire side of the room with tall wooden ones which when opened fully brought in plenty of sunshine & fresh air. The windows were covered with black out curtains. My desk was placed at an angle from the windows to give it maximum light. It was a custom designed piece with a quartz countertop. Behind the desk was a book case filled with books on interior design as well as fiction novels from some of my favorite authors. On the other side of the desk, I had opted for 2 comfortable lounge chairs as opposed to office chairs to make the setup seem cozier. An upholstered sofa, a large coffee table & a chaise lounge on the other side of the room offered an even more inviting setting for my clients. Paintings of my choosing from scenic watercolors to bold portraits were hung at strategic vantage points & various light fixtures provided mood lighting. There was a coffee machine near the desk with a mini-fridge – perfect for when I had to work late or spend the night to finish up the designs. A washroom in the corner completed the set-up.

"Wow!" said Vinay admiringly as he sat down on the sofa "looking at your office today I think my apartment can surely use some décor. All I have managed are the bare essentials. Did you pick out everything here?"

"Yes. The furniture is a hodge podge of stuff I found & then refurbished & the paintings are from my friends who are artists" I replied pleased that he had liked my space.

"So how expensive is it to hire a designer" he enquired

"That depends on the project." I replied with a smile as I placed the lilies on my desk & picked a vase to fill it with water from the wash basin. "These are indeed very beautiful" I sincerely offered.

"Generally, the client gives us a budget & a list of things they want in the space. We then work around that. I have a regular contractor who has been with me since I started Parampara. I make the designs with the 3 D software that I use. Then my contractor & his team bring those designs to life" I said with a smile enjoying explaining my work to Vinay.

"Wow! That does sound interesting. I will definitely have to get you to agree on designing my apartment" Vinay declared looking at me as I arranged the lilies.

"Veena, will you have dinner with me sometime?" He asked out of the blue.

I looked up from my arrangement "Don't you think you are coming on a little too strong?" I asked though I was quite flattered by the question.

"When I like someone, I tend to come on strong. But if you feel I am pressurizing you then I will back off" offered Vinay & I immediately regretted my words.

"Dinner sounds nice but actually, I wanted to ask you if it was ok for me to attend the Shok Sabha...with you" I said remembering the news article & deciding to take advantage of the dinner invite

"Mr. Khanna's shok Sabha?" asked Vinay narrowing his eyes.

"Yes. I want to offer my condolences to his family" I continued "and I thought that maybe we could go together? I could be a good cover for you to ask your questions don't you think?"

Vinay regarded me thoughtfully & then asked

"Why do really you want to go?" I understood that the detective in him would not allow him to take me at face value.

"I read in the newspaper that Mr. Khanna is survived by his wife, Mrs. Pinky Khanna, who was a small-time actress before her marriage to Mehul. The article also mentioned that he has 2 children. Believe it or not I just want to meet the family of the man whose death occurred in front of my eyes" I hurriedly finished refusing to make eye contact.

"Hmm... You seem to have done your research on the family. Are you sure this has nothing to do with the feeling that you had right before he died?" asked Vinay looking at me expectantly

"If I told you, it did would you believe me?" I challenged.

"Veena I am a lifelong student of science. My profession doesn't allow me to take flights of fancy. In my line of work, I have seen the extent to which people can go when they believe they can get something through magic. It is a dark path indeed" Vinay said sincerely.

I could understand his skepticism. Belief in magic could indeed turn good people on a dark path. But magic itself was not good or bad. The one who wielded it decided that. I hoped that Vinay would come to see it in time.

"Having said that I have also first-hand experienced people who had feelings which saved their lives. Be it avoiding travel on a certain day or choosing one path over another" continued Vinay as he looked at me appraisingly. "We can go together. But Veena don't get involved with the investigation. These are not good people" he warned as he got up to leave.

"What about coffee?" I asked as he started to leave

"Some other time. I never thought I would spend so much time admiring any space. Your office is indeed beautiful Veena. But now I need to reach the station. Can I take a rain check?" he asked glancing at the watch

"Ok sure" I said shrugging my shoulders.

As he turned around & left, I realized that my earring was still with Vinay. Either he had forgotten to give it or it was an excuse for yet another meeting. Knowing Vinay, I knew it was the latter & I felt pleased.

I made myself a cup of coffee & proceeded to check my emails. Later in the day, I planned to head to the gallery to select more frame options for Charmie. I had tie-ups with most of the suppliers & had worked with the same contractor for 3 years now which meant that he could now understand & execute my designs with almost 90% accuracy. This brought down the need for my supervision at the site considerably freeing my time to bring in more clients. Thanks to the timely deliveries & quality of work I had built up an enviable client base in a short time.

Charmie's place would give me direct entry into a whole new league & hence I had avoided taking on any new clients till it was completed. After the paintings were reframed (if at all needed) & the light fixtures were fitted, all I needed was a spectacular wallpaper for the foyer & Charmie's unit would be ready for handover. While I would have preferred to wait for Anil's response on the frames first, I was working with a tight timeline. Hence, I had decided to get options beforehand. If there was a problem, I would switch out the frames with one of the other options. We were already on Thursday & I could wait another 72 hrs. to catch up with Anil. Sundays were only for family at the Poonawala household so I was quite sure I would catch him then. The timeline I had committed for completion & handover still a couple of weeks away but in my line of business I have observed, it is always good to have a buffer.

After checking my emails, I had a video call with my contractor Prakash Shah who assumed me that things were progressing as planned. I then called the gallery to check if the new frames I had seen on their website were in stock & could I come down to see them. The gallery owner informed me that it would take a couple of hours for the frames to be delivered to their showroom from the warehouse. This meant that I had some time to kill. I decided to try & actively call Mr. Khanna's ghost. I figured he had some explaining to do regarding his 'business dealings' & maybe seeing me speaking with Vinay & getting to know about his other activities is what was causing him to stay away.

As I was taught by my grandmother, I first shut the black out curtains & sat down cross legged in the middle of the floor on the other side of my desk. I then put on my noise cancelling earphones to shut out the outside sounds. I concentrated on my breathing to center myself inhale- exhale-inhale- exhale. Once all my senses were sharpened, I called to the magic building within me & channeled it outwards calling out to the ghost of Mr. Khanna. The magic flared but instead of the ghostly form materializing, I felt my magic slam against a wall. Since I had never actively summoned a ghost before this, I tried once again thinking maybe I was doing something wrong. This time I allowed my magic to build some more before channeling it. I felt minor cracks in the magical wall that seemed to be keeping my magic at bay. I figured I would be able to break down the resistance by exerting even more magic but before I could attempt again, the doorbell of the office rang.

"I was nearby for a client meeting & thought I would drop in to discuss," said Anil. "You know how hyper Charmie can get better to get this out of the way before I return home tonight" he continued with a tired smile as he stepped into the office.

"Sure. Would you like a cup of coffee?" I asked to which he simply nodded.

"I like the frames & the paintings & the bed linen. I like all of it but how much excitement is a man supposed to show at the end of a tiring day? Every day?" Anil was asking me. "Now if I tell her that I like the frames she won't believe me & will think I am just saying it to flatter her or to save money. What should I do?" Anil asked me.

This was indeed something that would have to be tackled carefully considering the couple dynamics between Anil & Charmie. I thought about it for some time & replied handing Anil a cup of coffee.

"Take her out for dinner tonight. Call her right now & invite her for a dinner like you used to when you were dating. Also tell her that since she has taken so much effort decorating your home & since you have not been able to participate as much, you have taken time out & chosen the perfect frames for her paintings. You see Charmie took down the frames when you didn't give her a reaction & then she went & dumped them back at the gallery in her car. The frames are all wooden carving frames which I had gotten painted a deep forest green to contrast with your white walls. I wanted to give them a slightly antique look by brushing on gold highlights but Charmie wanted to check with you first. I will simply go to the gallery finish the gold highlights & have them delivered & hung at your place before you return from the movie. You can tell Charmie that those are the frames you chose. If you play it right, she won't notice that they are the same ones. It won't cost you extra & will save me a lot of time & effort" I said.

"That is brilliant Veena. Let me call her right away" exclaimed Anil as he finished his coffee & dashed out of my office.

"Remember you are asking her out on a date. Don't be in a hurry." I yelled after him.

"I won't" he replied as I smiled at one more crisis being solved.

I had one more cup of coffee with the chocolate chip cookies which I had a stash of in my office but this did not satiate my hunger. I needed food do I decided to grab a sandwich on my way to the gallery. It was well past afternoon & if I was to keep my promise to Anil, I would have to paint or antique the frames myself in the time I had. All I needed now to complete the space was the wallpaper but after visiting numerous stores & browsing through endless catalogs, I was still not able to find anything that caught my eye. As I was shutting down my laptop, I noticed the illustration of the family tree that a prospective client had shared with me to be framed & I had an inspired idea – What if I got a custom wallpaper made of the Poonawala family tree for the main living space & switched the wall paper chosen for that space to the foyer? It would give the Wow factor I wanted if done tastefully. I needed reference images. With that thought in mind, I left the office.

Chapter 8 – Date night

The next day I had decided to work from home as I had some calls scheduled with vendors & I wanted to create some design options for the wallpaper. I had worked late the previous night & had no opportunity to contact Mr. Khanna's ghost again after my failed attempt. I planned to try again today after finishing with the wallpaper design. My main workspace at home was a work desk in one corner of my room near the window. All my inspo was tacked to the wall above.

The layout of our house is pretty standard. It is an old house passed down through the generations. Varsha's & my bedrooms are upstairs while the common areas & the master as well as a 4th bedroom are on the ground floor. The house also has a basement which first belonged to my mother but now my Nani uses. The first-floor bedrooms also have an independent access which works well for me considering that I kept pretty odd hours. It also gave me independence. Varsha's bedroom is at the other end & we share a bathroom which is a source of squabbles every morning. While the ground floor had been designed as per the tastes of my parents, our floor is a hodge podge of 2 completely different styles as Varsha's tastes are completely different from my own. My bedroom is light & airy with pastel colors & gold highlights in the antique bedside lamps & my full-length mirror (an antique which I happened to find in our attic & restored). Varsha's room has bold purples & bright yellows mixed in with tints of black but the overall effect is pretty striking.

Before starting on the wallpaper design, I called up Charmie & asked her to send the names for the family tree both on her side as well as on Anil's side. I spent the whole morning making mockups of 3-4 designs & by afternoon, I had sent across my design ideas to Charmie. As I was about to head down for my lunch break, Varsha flounced into my room wearing my new forest green dress & started twirling in front of the mirror. I was pointedly ignoring her & trying to tamp down my anger.

The moment she spotted me she put on her best fake smile & said “Oh Di you are so sweet! Please don’t be angry. I got so many compliments for my dress.”

“You mean my dress don’t you Varsha? The same Forest green dress that I bought as a treat for myself? I hadn’t even worn that dress”

“But Di you did try it & you said the color did not suit you. Remember?” said Varsha innocently.

“So what? that does not give you the right to pull it out of my wardrobe & wear it to your retarded friend’s birthday party!” I yelled getting angrier by the minute.

“Reema is not retarded.” Varsha responded hotly.

“Of course, you won’t think she is retarded Varsha. The girl worships the ground you walk on. She barely manages to pass & her only aspiration in life seems to be to find a rich husband.” I said remembering my last interaction with Reema.

“Speaking of husbands, any updates on Vinay?” asked Varsha

“Do not try to change the subject Varsha. You are not allowed to wear my dress before me.”

“Di, you do not even like the dress. Besides, you have already removed the tags because you cannot try on a garment with 3 tags on it – your words not mine. So, you certainly can’t return it”

“Well, I have a super sensitive skin can you blame me? I can understand a garment having one tag but what is the need to have 3 of them on the same piece of clothing? Is it so that the attendants can play rummy with the discarded tags after billing?” I asked getting flustered – so many tags & packing materials in my opinion were harming our planet as much as the plastic wastes.

“Oh Di, you are so funny”

“It’s not funny Varsha no one cares about the environment anymore.” I said with a sigh

“My di! the lone crusader for the environment.”

“Do not try to butter me sister dear. You can have this dress but you owe me a new one.” I was not willing to let go on this.

"Ok! Let me get my pocket money & I will buy you one. You know I don't earn as yet." Said Varsha making a puppy dog face.

"I know that the moment you get your pocket money you will spend it on the new camera lens you have been wanting forever. I also know that our Bua has given you Shagun envelope to cover her marriage anniversary photo shoot so hand that over Varsha. I even know where you have put the envelope" I said jumping over the bed towards Varsha's room.

"No way Di. I am not giving you that money" said Varsha as she blocked my path & I started tickling her.

Varsha's passion was photography & in addition to her bachelor's course she was also taking extra classes on photography. All her pocket money was spent on new photography equipment. So, getting my hands on the Shagun envelope was important for me.

"How about I give you something in lieu of the dress di?" asked Varsha as I continued to tickle her.

"And what would that be?" I asked. In spite of the age difference, Varsha & I were the same size & that effectively doubled our wardrobe. Except Varsha seemed to like my clothes more than her own.

"I will let you wear my red skirt & white peasant top for your first date with Vinay," said Varsha.

"How do you know I have a date?" I asked as Varsha enlarged her eyes to comical proportions –

"You mean he actually asked you for a date? Wow! That guy sure moves fast & you are blushing. Good catch Di" said Varsha giving me a high five.

Incidentally the previous evening Vinay had called & we planned to go for a movie tonight. Technically it was our first official date & I was a little nervous which was new for me.

"Ok. But the skirt is just a loan. I still want a new dress" I said prissily.

"Whateves..." said Varsha "I think we should check out the haunted cottage near Glocal Junction Di. That is what I wanted to tell you before you pounced on me for 'borrowing' your dress. If there is any evidence, I have a feeling it will be there at the cottage"

Varsha was still admiring the dress. Since the time I had told her about the murder, she had been obsessed with the cottage. I had seen her doing some online research about the owners- the Gadres's. Early on I had realized that Varsha's gut feelings were solid but I wanted to try & call the ghost one more time before visiting the cottage. When I told Varsha about my experience with the magical wall, she suggested us trying to call the ghost together to which I readily agreed.

Once again, we closed the curtains & the 2 of us sat cross legged on the floor of my bedroom facing each other. We held hands & closed our eyes. Varsha's magic was different than mine & she had even lesser practice using it as my father had stopped out magic lessons after Ma's death. This time the spell we cast had a different effect. I was suddenly pulled in a dark room which looked like some sort of a storage unit. I felt intense hatred but also fear as I moved around in the space. Every time I tried to leave from the room, I experienced intense pain & was back where I had started. Just then the door opened & I saw the shadow of a woman but before her face could come into focus, magic slammed me back into my body. Both Varsha & I opened our eyes at the same time looking at each other incredulously. Either of us having no idea of what had happened. But one thing was certain- we needed guidance & there was only one person who could offer it – Nani.

After a futile search of the house which yielded no results, we concluded that Nani had gone AWOL. This was not alarming though & quite a regular occurrence in the Pardeshi household. Nani refused to carry a mobile or answer it when she didn't want to in spite of Baba asking her many times. She said it infringed on her privacy. As per Nani our magic kept us connected & if there was danger, it would guide us to each other. Concluding that she had probably stepped out for one of her infamous excursions into the hills, I decided to have a quick visit with a prospective client who were looking to convert their garage into an apartment which they could rent while Varsha went to her photography classes. Nani never fully explained the purpose of these excursions to us & I presumed it had something to do with her wandering nature. She was a wild spirit at heart & preferred outdoors to the civilized world which seemed to be taking over the wilderness. These excursions were her attempts at rebellion but she always came back mostly within a few days.

The meeting for the garage conversion was with Mr. & Mrs. Gupta who were both senior citizens. They both welcomed me & showed me around the space. We concluded the meeting with me promising that the space could indeed be made habitable & I would be visiting again with my contractor to give them approximate costing & making my designs. Since the meeting had gone on longer than I expected, I had to hurry back home. I had had barely had enough time to change when Vinay arrived. He had reached at exactly 7 pm, to pick me up from my house for our movie date making me feel guilty for my tardiness & my hastily applied makeup. Vinay was driving a Volkswagen which was unfortunate as it would provide more fodder to Mrs. Joshi who was at the window seemingly cleaning the grains in the plate but in reality, keeping a watch on the neighborhood. I waved at her as I exited the house letting her know that I was very much aware of her true intentions.

"So, Mr. Vinay Verma who are you?" I asked as I sat in the shiny new car that Vinay was driving.

I was sure seeing Vinay & the car was the highlight of the day for Mrs. Joshi. She would continue to stare at us through the window till we left. "And since when can honest police officers afford a Volkswagen?"

I asked teasingly ignoring the pointed stare of my neighbor. Vinay was a little annoyed as he looked at me.

"The car was a gift from my father. He is the mayor of Pune" replied Vinay nonchalantly.

I was shocked on hearing this.

"Oh! So you are that Verma" I asked sheepishly. "Tum to bahut hi amir nikle. (Wow! You are indeed rich) I feel like Geet from Jab we met. Have you seen the movie" I asked trying to lighten the mood.

"Sure. It is one of my favorites" said Vinay though he seemed a bit tense.

"So do you want to run away from the city & live in the hills with me Mr. Verma?" I sked channeling Geet to get him to relax. I knew I had touched a nerve.

Vinay seemed to realize what I was doing & gave me a slight smile. "Just as soon as we find Mr. Khanna's murderer we will go for a holiday in the hills Ms. Pardeshi" he replied.

Seeing his dimple come out to play caused my stomach to do mini flip flops. I was glad he was letting go of the stupidity of my question.

"You should definitely wear a disguise the next time you come to pick me up" I said

"You mean because of that old aunty who keeps staring at us?" he asked

"That is Mrs. Joshi & she is the biggest gossip of our society. If she comes to know you are the mayor's son, she won't limit herself to watching from the window. She will come out & insist on talking to you & then you are on your own" I said

"Oh, she can't be that bad," said Vinay

"Trust me she is. She will tell you in no uncertain terms what your father is doing wrong & how things need to change." Vinay was amused at my response.

"Guess I will take your word for it then. I will find a pair of dark glasses & a wig. Will that work?"

"No"

I said & both of us burst out laughing imagining him sneaking around wearing a horrendous disguise.

"So how does a politician's son end up as a policeman?" I asked trying to get a handle on my date.

"I am a detective" said Vinay "my father wanted me to become an IAS officer but I was more interested in being on the field than at sitting behind a desk."

"Wasn't he disappointed that you chose a different line of work?" I asked curious to the father-son dynamics.

"I think he was a little, but father is not in politics for the power. He actually wants to serve the people & make a difference. I told him that is exactly what I would be doing though in a different manner" said Vinay though I felt there was something he was holding back. "What about you? Why interior designing?" he asked trying to shift the conversation to me.

"I love making every space beautiful. You must have gauged from my house that it is a pretty old bungalow."

"Yes, but it has been updated beautifully, "said Vinay.

"There is a story there. Are you up for hearing it" I asked Vinay curiously

"I am always up for a good story" he enthusiastically replied

"When I was a kid, I used to hate living in that bungalow." I began "It was very dark & dingy. It was my Nani's house which was given to her by her grandmother but she never stayed in it. When my mother got married, she & my father shifted into the bungalow & my Nani continued to stay in her house which was at the outskirts of the city. I used to pester my mother to sell our bungalow & move to a new building. Getting tired of my constant complaints, my father hired an interior designer to come & update the place. That guy for me was a magician. He turned our bungalow from an ugly duckling to a swan. Seeing how happy everyone was when the work was finished, I decided that is what I wanted to pursue." I finished

"I am sure your mother would also have been very happy with the newly renovated house," said Vinay

"Ma...Ma passed away before she could see the changes," I said choking back the sob which threatened to escape every time I told someone about my mother.

Though it had been over a decade, my mother's memories were still fresh in my mind. It was always painful to talk about her death.

"I am sorry. I didn't realize your mother had passed away" said Vinay apologetically.

"You couldn't have, could you? I never told you. Anyway a few years after Ma's death Nani moved in with us & she has been harassing all of us ever since" I chuckled

"You mean taking care of you right" asked Vinay confusion evident on his face

"Sure. That is what she will have you believe. But you have to meet her to understand what I am saying" I replied "My Nani is unique."

"Well, I never thought of design as transformative but I think for you the changes would have been a welcome distraction after the loss you were forced to face at such a young age"

Vinay was speaking in a serious voice & I realized that may be what he was trying to say was true. The transformation of our house had come about when all of us as a family had suffered an irrevocable loss. Without Ma it would have been impossible for us to reside in the same house where every nook & cranny was filled with her memories. Especially for my father who had first entered the Vaastu as a new husband. I admired Vinay's fortitude for being able to understand the role that that renovation had played in my life. He was looking at me intently trying to gauge my reaction to his words.

"Yes. We don't talk about it much- Ma's death I mean" I said shrugging as I tried to change the topic

"If you don't mind me asking, how did she die" asked Vinay.

"It was an accident. Varsha & I were in school. We never got to see her after..." I said looking away.

"I am really sorry. I can see this is not a subject for a first date. I hope you still want to go for the movie & not punch me for spoiling your mood?" asked Vinay mischievously as we pulled into the parking lot of the theatre. I nodded a little overwhelmed.

The movie we had chosen for our first date was not a romantic one but rather the latest in the Avenger series which both of us liked. It kind of married our interests – the crime fighting & the supernatural. After the movie we decided to have Mastanis which was the fancy name Pune had come up with for a concoction of milkshake with ice-cream. It was November & the weather was quite chilly. As we were strolling to the ice-cream parlor, I was reconsidering my outfit choice for the evening. The peasant top was thin & though my skirt was long, I was cold. Vinay noticed this & promptly offered me his jacket which in turn left him only with his shirt but when I declined the jacket saying he needed it, he scowled at me & draped it over my shoulders. I was touched by this thoughtful gesture.

Just as we reached the ice-cream parlor, Vinay got a call from an unknown number. He excused himself & asked me to place his order. I was on my second sundae when he returned.

"Sorry Vinay. I finished your Mastani else the ice-cream would have melted. Let's order a new one for you" I said grinning. I loved ice cream & especially the Chocolate one was my favorite. Vinay smiled at me & wiped away the chocolate mustache from my lips. The gesture natural, though the touch of his fingers on my face left me breathless.

"Sure Veena. I will place the order for my Mastani. Do you want one more?" he asked teasing me. I shook my head as I continued to sip the last of my milkshake.

"I got a very strange phone call from Nemina right now." Informed Vinay as he came back from the counter having placed the order. “The girl from the restaurant that disappeared ...” he looked at me questioningly

“Yes, I remember her. Were you able to trace her?” I asked remembering that the police had neither her address nor her contact number.

“We did manage to trace her but she refused to talk to the police asking us to communicate with her lawyer instead” I could gauge the frustration in Vinay’s voice “... and now she called me out of the blue. You will never believe what she asked... She told me that the only way she would talk to me is if you were present at the time of questioning” he continued & the bewilderment he felt was apparent on his face “Of course, she didn’t mention you by name but she did mention that she wanted the lady at the next table who had yelled after the murder.” He looked at me with an unasked question

“I don’t know her Vinay” I said “If that is what you wanted to know. In fact, I saw her for the first time at the restaurant”

Vinay seemed to be lost in thought for some time. When he spoke, it was with resignation

“I knew that you don’t know her, Veena. We did a background check on her. Still, it is a very odd request to make so I had to ask. I had asked you to not get involved with the investigation but I need to speak with Nemina. Would you mind too much accompanying me? I will take full responsibility of your safety”.

Looking at the solemn expression on Vinay’s face I wanted to tease him a bit, but truth be told I was more than a little curious at the strange demand myself so I agreed. Vinay immediately called back on the same number & fixed a place & time for the meeting promising me that we would be going together.

Chapter 9 – Funeral

"Everyone knows you are supposed to wear black to a funeral" said Varsha as she stepped into my room

"Only if you are in England & the last, I checked we are firmly in India." I replied exasperated

"So what? The color you are wearing is definitely not what you should be wearing" she said sticking out her tongue

"Oh & since when are you an authority on funeral attire" I asked Varsha humoring her. "Have you seen any of your favorite Bollywood stars sporting black at a funeral Varsha?"

I knew I had her there. The newspapers regularly covered the who's who of Bollywood decked in their finest white chikankari suits sarees & kurtas with their goggles for the funeral of any celebrity & my sister was a die-hard fan of the movies.

"But this is not even white Di" pouted Varsha.

"It's close enough" I said glancing for one last time at my ice blue chikankari suit. "Besides why are you obsessing over my attire? Don't you have better things to do?" I asked curiously "For that matter how come you are home at this hour?"

"I was just bored. Besides our portion is already completed. Can I come with you Di?" asked Varsha

"Absolutely not! I am myself an uninvited guest. I can't ask Vinay to take both of us" I said in a stern voice

"Whateves... maybe I will hang out with Nani then" she said blowing a raspberry.

Nani had come back last night after 2 days of absence & had not woken up as yet. If Varsha thought waking her up this early then God help her. (It was 10 am but my Nani was a late sleeper & when asked she would give her Rakshasa heritage as a reason for sleeping in late since typically, we were known to be predominantly night creatures)

Today was the Shok sabha & I was going with Vinay to offer my condolences to the family or at least that is what I would have to pretend to do. In Nani's absence Varsha & I had tried to do some research on our own but the only satisfactory explanation that we had come up with for our experience with 'ghost summoning' was that somehow the joining of our magic had enabled us to see the physical space that the ghost seemed to have been trapped in. Since we could not freely discuss about magic with my father around, we were waiting for Nani to return to answer all of our questions. I had also been busy on the work front trying to get everything in order for the handover date & juggling to make time for new designs for prospective clients. The murder investigation was keeping Vinay occupied but we spoke regularly & met for coffee as often as our schedules allowed. Vinay was spending hours going through all of Mr. Khanna's clients in the past 5 yrs. He was convinced there was something he was missing. It was a tedious task to undertake. But so far, the police had not uncovered any new or conclusive information. Vinay was hoping that would change today when he could talk face to face with some of Mehul's business associates. They had been avoiding him by directing the police to their lawyers. While Vinay was busy chatting with Mehul's associates, I had planned to observe all the people who would be present for the funeral to check if I could find the murderer.

In a very short span of time, Vinay and I had become more than just two people in each other's lives. We talked every day, sharing the highs and lows of our lives. This plan for the funeral – split & gather information had also been discussed in one such conversation. Our conversations were like a safe haven, a place where we could be ourselves without any pretence. The mundane details of our days were just as important as the deeper thoughts we shared. We had a rhythm, a comfort in each other's presence that made every conversation feel like coming home. When we managed to meet in person, it was a different kind of joy. Whether it was over a cup of coffee or a meal, the chemistry between us was electric. The way he looked at me, the subtle touches, and the unspoken understanding spoke volumes about the depth of our feelings. My day felt incomplete unless I had narrated every little bit of it to Vinay.

But underneath the surface of our blossoming relationship, I harboured a fear—the fear of unveiling my true identity as a Rakshasi. The thought of letting Vinay in on this secret filled me with anxiety. Would he see me differently? Would he be scared away? Our connection which was a source of strength for me, a place where I felt cherished and understood would it be strong enough to withstand this test? As we navigated the twists and turns of our relationship, I wondered if the day would come when I could gather the courage to reveal the truth to him, hoping that our feelings for each other could withstand the challenges that lay ahead.

It had been exactly 4 days from the date of the murder but after the last attempt Varsha & I had made, Mr. Khanna's ghost has been uncontactable. I was used to the ghosts beating down my door (in a manner of expression) till they got what they wanted but these circumstances were very unusual. The only new information I had was the autopsy results which Vinay had shared with me on our first date. Apparently, Mr. Khanna's cause of death was very unusual. It looked like he had suffocated but there was no visible obstruction in his airways. They had also tested for poisons but the medical examiner had so far been unable to identify what exactly had killed him. Vinay himself was confused as he had assumed that it would be an easily traceable poison. The other thorn in his side was proving to be Mrs. Pinky Khanna who had taken to calling him at all hours of the day asking him about the progress & requesting him to visit her with updates daily. Vinay's guess, that this murder had been committed by a former client of Mr. Khanna seemed to be the only plausible lead for the police, but without evidence everyone was a suspect & yet no one was a suspect! This included the widow as well who was left with a considerable insurance but no inheritance. Overall, we needed a lot more information to proceed.

My agenda for today was to dig as much information as I could from the people at the funeral & try to find the ghost; if he was hanging out at home. Some ghosts tended to do that as it was their comfort zone. I applied my favorite lipstick which was so subtle it looked like I was wearing no makeup. I knew I looked very good in the suit but it wouldn't do to wear makeup to a funeral. I was just about ready when the doorbell rang.

"Hello, it's Varsha I presume" I could hear Vinay's voice in the living room.

"Hello Mr. Detective. Wow! You are really handsome. Di will be right down. She was waiting for you."

I could hear Varsha talking to Vinay. Oh! I could kill her! Why did she have to stick her nose in my business? I quickly sprayed on some of my favorite perfume (no one needs to smell bad at a funeral) & went down.

"So, this is the guy solving that murder" I could hear Nani's voice before I reached so she must have woken up.

"Yes Nani," said Vinay

"I am Veena's Nani not yours. You can call me Mrs. Nalini Desai" she said as Vinay looked at me amused at the choice of words. "You are better looking than most of the other policemen I have seen & why aren't you in uniform" she continued

"Actually, I am a detective Ma'am. We don't need uniforms" Vinay answered chuckling "though I do get asked that question a lot".

"Oh, I see. Can you not call me Ma'am though? It just makes me feel very old. Mrs. Desai will do" Nani said graciously "Since Veena seems to like you, I think it is my duty to invite you for a family dinner. Does 2 days from now work for you?"

Nani had essentially thrown a googly & I was anxious of Vinay's response. Thankfully my father had already left for office. He was a CA

& worked at a private firm. If Baba were around, he would have probably had palpitations knowing that Nani was inviting a guy – a police detective no less to have dinner at our house. After the last disastrous dinner with Sarthak, my father seemed to have taken a tentative break from the 'Find a groom for Veena' agenda which was working in my favor. Vinay though seemed tickled with the invite

"Sure Mrs. Desai. I will make time for this dinner. I look forward to it" he said.

As we were leaving the house, Mrs. Joshi approached me. There was no way I could avoid her. She stood directly in our path

"Veena, can you please ask your friends to not trample over my flower bed?" she said without any preamble

"Huh... did you trample over the flowers Vinay?" I asked looking at him; a bit confused with Mrs. Joshi's accusation.

"Not him" she said annoyed like it was my fault for not knowing

"It was a girl". This was news for me. None of my friends had recently visited my house.

"Did she give you a name" I asked Mrs. Joshi

"Are you daft girl? Why would I ask her name? I just yelled at her from my window to stop trampling my bushes as she strolled around your house"

The houses in our society were all bungalows. They were not separated by walls but rather by fences or simply bushes. Since each bungalow had a yard the distance between the houses was quite large. The only reason I could think of for someone to have been walking on Mrs. Joshi's bushes was that they could see the magical wards. This was interesting.

"Can you describe her Ma'am?" asked Vinay sensing that something was not adding up from my expression.

"Oh! Don't call me Ma'am. I am Hemlata... Mrs. Hemlata Joshi. I am Veena's neighbor almost like a distant Aunt. Isnt that right beta... tell him no" she said looking at me.

That was two women who had had told Vinay not to address them as ma'am in a span of less than an hour. Seeing Vinay's face, I was having a hard time holding in my laughter.

"Umm... yes I have known Mrs. Joshi for a long time" I said rolling my eyes at Vinay behind Mrs. Joshi's back.

"And who is this guy dear?" asked Mrs. Joshi as she appraisingly looked at Vinay.

"He is just a friend" I said purposely not divulging any details.

"Well, he sure looks like he could soon become more than a friend right Veena? Don't forget about my nephew otherwise" said Mrs. Joshi & I was horrified at her outspokenness

"You were describing the girl who trampled over your flower beds" interjected Vinay in an amused voice

"Oh yes! she seemed about Veena's age though she was dressed much better than Veena usually does. Seemed like she was going for some party but the cleavage was a bit much" said Mrs. Joshi wrinkling her nose in distaste.

"Nemina" both Vinay & I said simultaneously.

"I hope she is not some anti-social element" asked Mrs. Joshi looking in turn at both of us "else I will ask our society guard to be on the lookout for her"

"That is not needed aunty" I said hurriedly before Vinay could respond "I do know her. Just not that she had come for a visit. I must have been out then"

"May be. But I must insist that you ask all your friends to stay on your side of the fence" said Mrs. Joshi doubtfully as she walked back to her house.

As we got into the car, Vinay looked thoughtful. "Maybe you should ask the security guard to inform you if Nemina decided to pay another visit. I don't understand why she would stalk you like that" he said a bit worriedly.

"She has already agreed to meet us. What if she changes her mind because of this?" I asked "Don't you want to question her? Besides she looks harmless" I added though if she was magical, she would not be as innocent as I was painting her to be but I couldn't voice that out loud to Vinay.

After a short drive during which Vinay showered me with compliments on everything from my outfit to my jewelry, we arrived at the bungalow belonging to the Khannas. A huge placard with Mehul's photo on it confirmed that we were at the right place. As I got down from the car, I eyed the bungalow. It was opulent but comfortable. From the design it looked like it had either been recently built or recently renovated by someone with good taste. There was a winding driveway & on one side there was a car park while a carefully manicured lawn with beautiful flowering plants flanked the other side of the driveway. There were 3 cars parked in the garage. The main entrance was accessed through a short flight of stairs. Vinay handed over the car to the valet making me realize that the owners had probably arranged for parking in a nearby lane and the 3 parked cars probably belonged to the owners themselves. There was a soothing music playing as we entered the main living room. The photo of Mr. Sharma in a huge golden photo frame was placed on one side of the room while the people who had come to offer their condolences were split with the ladies on one side & the gents on the other side.

A beautiful woman with layers of carefully applied makeup was sitting near the photo wearing a white chikankari saree just like in the movies. So much for no makeup at a funeral! I could see now that Mehul had a type – beautiful women with lots of makeup! All that was left to complete this one's look was the dark goggles. The people coming in were offering their condolences to her. It was the widow I presumed- Mrs. Pinky Khanna. The same woman who had been pestering Vinay on the phone, calling him every day to get updates on the case. After seeing her, my assumption was that she liked what she saw & was simply bidding her time till she made her move on Vinay. On the other side of the photo sat 2 kids. The son was around 4 yrs old while the daughter was a teenager & was dressed in a white salwar suit. The widow did not look old enough to have a daughter that old. Then I remembered reading online that the daughter was from an earlier marriage. The first Mrs. Khanna had died a few years earlier & Mehul had then married a starlet & had a son. From all the reading I had done on the Khanna family, the only person I didn't spot was Mehul's father.

As I was scanning the crowd, I felt uneasy as if someone's eyes were on me, the hairs on my hands stood on end. I turned & noticed that the daughter was keenly observing me. Her name was Maisha – something that was mentioned in the obituary while the son was called Sanish. When I met Maisha's gaze, she quickly averted her eyes. Vinay nudged me & I noticed that we had arrived at the side of Mrs. Khanna who was clasping Vinay's arms & bending such that Vinay had a direct view of her ample cleavage. He was nudging me to get him out of her grip. In spite of the situation, I felt like giggling. I sent a small jolt of magic which caused Pinky's grabby hands to get a small jolt of electricity & for her to withdraw them from Vinay's biceps. As Pinky started adjusting her saree probably mistaking the jolt for static, I saw Maisha giving her an extremely annoyed look. I found the dynamics between the 2 women quite interesting but before I could ponder on that I found that Pinky's eyes were now scanning my face waiting for me to introduce myself.

"My heartfelt condolences to you Mrs. Khanna" I said attempting a half hug. "I was with Mr. Khanna, your husband in the restaurant when he collapsed."

Pinky's eyes narrowed & I could feel her getting angry. Just as she was about to launch herself at me, Vinay interrupted;

"What she means is she was at the next table with her friend when your husband died." I understood my mistake a split second too late.

Pinky probably knew her husband's penchant for dining his girlfriends in expensive restaurants & she had assumed I was one of them. Vinay's words seemed to calm down Mrs. Khanna & she once again started sobbing softly in her handkerchief. After offering our condolences, Vinay & I made our way to the lawn. There sitting on a table was a very old gentleman who was being helped into a chair by a man servant.

"That is Mr. Khanna's father" Vinay whispered in my ear. "Will you be ok by yourself for a little while? There are a few people here that I want to talk to" he asked.

I nodded in agreement & Vinay walked away to talk to a group of gentlemen gathered in one corner of the garden. I continued observing the old man who seemed to be inconsolable.

'Mera beta... mujhe chod ke chala gaya. Ab is budhe ko koun sabhalega...' (My son is gone now who will look after this old man) he burst into huge sobs.

Just then Maisha stepped out. She spoke soothingly to her grandfather & started taking him inside the house towards the back presumably to his bedroom. For some reason I myself could not fully process, I decided to follow them. As I was observing the two, I saw the old man trip & fall. He was about to hit his head on the ground but Maisha supported him.

"Can't you watch where you are going old man? If anything happens to you it will just get blamed on me!" I couldn't believe what I had just heard. Maisha seemed to register my presence at that instant & immediately changed her demeanor.

"Oh! Old age has made you so clumsy."

She said sweetly trying to cover up but I could see it was all for my benefit. Then turning to me she offered a smile.

"Could you look after him for just a minute? I will get his doctor."

She turned & left before I could answer. The old man seemed to be scared & confused as he glanced around.

"I am Veena, uncle. I was in the same restaurant as your son when he died" I started. "Are you ok?"

The old man ignored me & started to shuffle towards one of the bedrooms. I presumed it was his room & started following him to ensure he did not fall again. He entered the bedroom & turned around to check if I was still following him. He then pointed to a photo on the wall. It seemed to be a family portrait but a dated one at that. It showed a boy of about 8 years posing with his parents.

"Is that you?" I asked the old man.

Before he could answer however Maisha returned with the doctor.

"What are you doing in my room?" she angrily asked me

"Your grandfather led me here" I replied surprised at her tone of voice.

"He must have gotten confused again. Doctor uncle can you check him please? He just tripped again" she said with irritation turning to the other man with her.

"Thank you so much for taking care of him. Now I think the doctor & I can manage." She told me. I was clearly being dismissed.

"No problem. I think he needs rest may be a sedative..." I said to the doctor as I left the room. I could feel Maisha's eyes on me the entire time I was walking out.

I started to search for Vinay to tell him about what I had witnessed. As I was wandering around in the crowd, I heard one of the women talking

"Did you hear what happened to Raghu?"

"Who is Raghu?" said another one

"He was Mr. Khanna's driver for the past 5 yrs. Quite an old man & he must have been pretty attached to Mehul," said the first woman

"So, one of the staff then" said the second woman dismissively "What happened to him?" she asked

"He had a paralytic attack the same night that Mr. Khanna died. In the parking lot of the restaurant itself. Apparently, the police went looking for him & found him in time else he may have died there!" said the first woman, conspiratorially.

This bit of information was news to me. I didn't know yet whether it was relevant to the case but I decided I would ask Vinay about it. Two deaths in the same vicinity at almost the same time seemed more than a coincidence. It was quite interesting listening to some of the neighbors gossiping about the nature of Mr. Khanna's business. All of them also thought he was murdered by one of his clients whom he had swindled; at least those were their surface thoughts. I also heard Mrs. Khanna's friends talking about her plight & wondering if she would be left penniless thanks to a prenup. While I was generally opposed to meddle in other people's business, eavesdropping was the only reason I had come to the funeral. The titbits of information I gathered here would prove to be useful later. After 30 mins of mingling in the crowd & listening to all the gossip, I ready to call it an evening. I had almost made up my mind to leave on my own when I spotted Vinay weaving his way through the crowd towards me. He seemed to be ducking his head periodically & when he reached me, he pulled me towards the door hiding behind the people milling about.

"What was that all about?" I asked Vinay once we were seated in his car "Did you see anyone you recognized?"

"No nothing like that I just did not want Pinky to catch sight of me. She kept grabbing me & asking me to stay near her in case she faints or something."

I started giggling.

"She doesn't seem so sad at her husband's death, does she? I mean genuinely sad. She seemed to be posing" I said

"Yes. I think so too but his passing has really affected his father & his daughter" replied Vinay.

"Well, no father wants his son to go before him so its justifiable" I continued "I am worried about the son. He is really young. He seemed kind of lost & his mother hardly seems in a condition to take care of him"

"I think she has always been that way. But Maisha will take care of him" said Vinay optimistically "Everyone I spoke with said that the brother & sister seem very close"

I suddenly felt an irrational fear for the boy remembering the way Maisha had behaved. But I decided to keep my thoughts to myself. This was indeed a very peculiar family with everyone having their own secrets & their own agendas.

"I hope we are able to close this case soon to give some closure to everyone in that family" I said.

"I hope so too provided we get some identifying cause of this death in the autopsy. I have asked them to do it again" said Vinay as I nodded in agreement. I was sure the second autopsy would be as inconclusive as the first one but I kept this too to myself. I realized that my omissions were piling up & that sooner rather than later this would drive a wedge between Vinay & me but I still did not think it was the right time to confide in him about magic. So, I kept quiet.

"Can we can have a quick lunch before I drop you" asked Vinay oblivious to my inner turmoil

"Sounds good" I said.

"Do you mind eating at "Glocal junction" again? We are very near & I love their Panner shaslik or has the murder spoilt the restaurant for you" Vinay was looking at me expectantly at this last bit.

"No, I love Paneer Shaslik as well" I said as I smiled at the relief on his face.

Actually, I would have said yes to anything at that point in time. My stomach was growling & I could practically see the soft paneer cubes in the creamy gravy served with the buttery herbed rice. The food was definitely distracting me from my earlier apprehensions.

"If you want, we can also order their sizzling brownie" said Vinay as if reading my thoughts

"With a scoop of vanilla ice-cream on top" I replied

"That would be perfect" he said with a smile

The atmosphere in the restaurant was more subdued than normal & the crowds too seemed to have reduced. While Vinay put it down to it being a weeknight, I had my doubts. The restaurant's business had definitely taken a hit after the murder. Vinay had told me that since Mr. Khanna was a regular at the restaurant, Vinay had taken the manager into confidence for his stakeouts. Though the restaurant was not as crowded there were still people at the bar. Most of them would be here for business & staying at the hotel itself I presumed.

The manager accompanied us seating us at the best table in the place. After handing us our menus, he politely enquired if he could speak in private with Vinay. Seeing his anxious expression, I nodded. Vinay stepped away from the table to have a chat with the manager while I placed our order. As I scanned all the tables in the restaurant, I was mentally retracing everything that had happened at the restaurant on that night – the sense of unease I felt, the red mist appearing out of nowhere, Nemina panicking & then Mr. Khanna collapsing. As I recollected the scene, I remembered something which I had overlooked previously. When Mehul collapsed, I had seen a small tattoo on the inside of his wrist which had been exposed. It was a symbol I had seen in one of the books my Nani carried around her. It was a magical symbol for protection.

Chapter 10 – Dark Musings

I was going to get a new lease of life. More power than I had ever anticipated. Her name as I had got to know was Veena. I had sensed her magic even before I came face to face with her. It called to me like nothing had before. The magic was old but born anew from what I could sense. It was a magic of the ancient world one I had only heard of, never seen. If she chose - if only she tapped into it, I would be no match for her power but before that I would devour her.

It was a shame that the power belonged to a girl who was barely using it from what I could see. She just went about her 'human' routine taking joy in the mundane & hanging out with that cop. Had I had such power I could finally stop pretending to be something I am not. Stop living in this pathetic human world.

Sometimes I wondered how these humans (& even some paranormals) surrounding me could be so stupid but perhaps it was not stupidity but humanity. The finiteness of their life probably forced them to live the way they chose to. Their emotions & their fragility kept them bound to a prison of their own making. I should know for I had encountered many such creatures – mostly men. Never had any of them believed in magic. Not even when I revealed to them exactly what I was - not even when the last breath was leaving their body could they see beyond my beauty. All of them the same as the man I had once called my husband. At a time when I was still human. He was the one that broke me. He ensured that I lost my humanity & in doing so sowed the seeds of his own demise. It was him & others like him who thought it was their god given right to decide the very purpose of my existence.

Now, decades later when all around me people claim that times have changed, I still see glimpses of the same men. They wear different- newer faces but I recognize them for what they are. They still consider it their right to decide the fate of others. I also see the reflections of the woman I was. These women have faces scarred fighting the ravages of men while some others reflecting the hopelessness of their existence. This is why I have never regretted my destiny.

My husband made me what I am but it was more humans- men like him who continued to sustain me. The women on the other hand were a different story. Even without knowing what I was they seemed wary of me – the wariness stemming more from my external beauty than the danger I could possess to them. Their pettiness was what had protected most of them, but not all for I could be charming if I chose to be & I was not picky when it came to my victims. Those few women though were a different story. They had fought with everything they possessed but ultimately, they were no match for me. There was only one whom I had willingly let go when she offered her husband in her place. Alas none of them had sufficed- neither the men nor the women. All my senses told me that the corruption of their souls was what was causing my powers to dwindle, none of them capable of providing the nourishment I sought.

This girl would turn the tables. Her mortal existence would be her ultimate undoing.

Chapter 11 – Inheritance

After dinner Vinay had dropped me home. Nani was fortunately at home when Vinay dropped me. I was eager to catch her up as we had barely spoken since she returned.

"So how was your visit to the funeral" asked Nani conversationally. She seemed to be in good spirits.

"I heard the Khannas have a really huge house." She exclaimed.

"Their house is beautiful. The lawns & the glass top terrace with the gym has given me new design ideas. But there is something I need your help on first, Nani" I said turning the conversation to my ghost.

"Something happened when you were gone. Varsha & I experimented with our magic..."

Nani's warm eyes held a mixture of surprise and understanding as I confessed to her what Varsha and I had attempted in her absence. She listened with rapt attention. Her expression was a mixture of concern and curiosity. Though I could also sense a hint of worry in her reaction, she held back. When I finished, she clutched my hands & exclaimed

"I am so glad that you girls actually used your magic for something other than parlor tricks!" Her gentle sigh carried a touch of amusement

She asked me to recite the incantations again & then said

"I think your conclusion is correct. There can be no other explanation. Since your magic could not bring the ghost to you, it took you to where Mehul's or Mr. Khanna's ghost has been trapped"

Then she turned thoughtful. as she emphasized

"Sit down, Veena, I think it's about time I told you about the importance of responsible magic. Let me tell you a story," Nani said, her voice carrying the weight of years gone by.

"Long ago, in a remote village in Konkan, there lived a young woman named Lila. Lila was a practicing Vaid (doctor practicing ayurveda) in the community. The other things she could do were known only to a few of the villagers. One day there was a murder in the village of a young boy of about 14-15. The body was found in the forest with ritualistic markings on it. The mother of the boy was insane with grief but the father wanted answers. This kind of thing was unheard of in the village. When the police did not take much interest in the case & concluded that the boy had probably been killed by an animal, his father approached Lila as he was aware of what she could do. Lila was a Rakshasi. She tried to call upon the ghost of the boy to know how he had died but was unable to summon him. Then she went to the place where his body was found. When she saw the markings made there, she realized that it was a human sacrifice. Lila then ventured into the forest. She felt a dark aura tainting the trees in the forest. Concealed behind a veil of darkness she discovered the markings of a witch! One who left no trace for the ordinary eye"

Nani had a flair for the dramatic however if I interrupted her or asked her to get on with the story, we would get into an argument which would take even more time so instead of saying anything I just nodded.

"The witch's desires were dark, her heart colder than the depths of winter. It was the witch who had convinced a humble farmer and his wife to aid her in killing the boy. She had promised them wealth beyond imagination in exchange for their cooperation. Blinded by greed, they had agreed"

Nani continued deepening her voice. Listening to this tale I could for the first time understand why Baba might abhor magic. I could only imagine the kind of grief that the boy's parents would have experienced. Varsha had just returned home as well & hearing the story, she immediately had joined us on the couch in the living room. Nani looked at her & continued.

"But that was not the end of the horrors for that family. The witch had trapped the soul of the boy & was using it as a slave. In addition, she was blackmailing the farmer who had committed the murder."

"Oh my god! That is horrible," said Varsha

"Yes beta, it is horrible indeed but many people still believe that sacrifice will get them what they want - be it wealth, progeny or success" said Nani with a sad look

"Unfortunately, the only people who benefit from such rituals are the ones who are born with the power & they almost always use it for dark purposes. Though as is usually the case, it was not the witch that committed the actual crime but human beings who were blinded by greed"

"Did she get away with it?" asked Varsha

"No. She didn't. Lila pursued the witch relentlessly, determined to put an end to her reign of terror. When their paths finally converged, a battle of magic and willpower ensued. The forest trembled as spells clashed and energies intertwined. In the end, it was Lila who emerged victorious, breaking the witch's malevolent hold and releasing the trapped soul of the young boy. Lila banished the witch & took the farmer to the police with enough evidence for them to arrest him. But she could not bring back the boy" Nani said.

"What happened to the boy's soul?" I asked.

"Once the witch was banished, her magical hold broke & the soul passed on to the other side" replied Nani

"And what about Lila?" asked Varsha

"Oh! She is very much alive. In fact, Lila is none other than my cousin Leelavati or Masi Nani as you girls know her." replied Nani.

Nani's eyes bore a mixture of sadness and resolve.

"Remember, Varsha, this tale serves as a reminder that power without restraint can lead even the strongest astray. It is our responsibility to wield magic wisely, for our choices ripple through time, shaping destinies for better or for worse"

Then she got very serious as she looked at me

"Veena, your great-aunt is a very powerful Rakshasi. I think what you are dealing with here also seems to indicate that this murder is magical" she continued. "And that the soul has definitely not passed over. The ghost is being controlled or more precisely your ghost has been trapped possibly by the one that killed him. Which also means Veena that you need to be very careful!".

"Be careful di. Don't underestimate the enemy or their sinister thoughts" said Varsha in a deep voice imitating Nani.

I think she was more shook up by the tale than she was willing to admit & this was her way of lightening the mood.

"Veena, ignore your sister. She probably doesn't realize it but just the way magic exists, so does malice. We don't know what was the motivation behind this murder but since the ghost reached out to you, we have to assume that now that the ghost is trapped, the murderer knows your identity. You can no longer be complacent dear. I need to teach you to protect yourself whether your father agrees or not" said Nani with determination.

We decided to start practicing in the basement late in the night so as to keep the lessons from Baba. I was not very comfortable with this but it would have to do for now to avoid a major confrontation between Nani & Baba.

Nani had told us that we would have to go to the basement for our first lesson at the stroke of midnight when my father would be fast asleep after a full day's work. Though tired, Varsha & I whispered excitedly as we descended into the basement. There was a sense of anticipation and awe in the air. While I had once been here as a child, Varsha had never been to this part of the house. This was my mother's sanctuary.

The steps were old and slightly creaky, reminding us that we were stepping into a realm of hidden wonders. The soft slant of moonlight had painted mysterious patterns on the floor as it entered through the antique windows original to the bungalow. There was a silvery glow all around us that seemed to dance with the shadows. Varsha and I exchanged excited glances, our eyes widening as we took in the scene before us. There were only 2 rooms in the basement though the basement was the footprint of the entire house. The larger room was open plan with tables & chairs scattered around while the entire space was lined with shelves. The smaller room in the corner though was locked. Both of us consciously ignored it. It was Ma's personal library. The whole of the basement had been designed by Ma & even us girls were seldom if ever allowed in here. Ancient tomes lined the shelves, their leather-bound spines whispering of untold knowledge and ancient secrets. I was sure Varsha heard the whispers too. The air was heavy with the scent of dried herbs and potions, creating an intoxicating blend that seemed to awaken the senses. Along with the books, colourful bowls adorned the shelves, each one holding its own story and purpose. Bright crystals caught the moonlight, scattering prismatic hues across the room, as if the very essence of magic was captured within their facets. Wooden boards etched with intricate markings and tokens lay in careful arrangement on the tables hinting at rituals and practices that spanned generations.

"Can you hear that Di?" whispered Varsha her eyes wide with astonishment

"Stop whispering girls. This is not high school or your college canteen" we heard Nani's voice before seeing her. Her steps were steady as she moved forward, her experienced hands lighting magical candles that added a soft, ethereal glow to the surroundings. I couldn't help but feel a sense of reverence as I took in the sight, realizing that we were standing on the threshold of a realm that few had the privilege to witness.

We couldn't help but explore more of this space. The soft illumination of the candles now revealed the intricate details of each artifact—the delicate brushstrokes on the bowls, the carefully inscribed symbols on the boards, and the timeless beauty of the ancient books that held the wisdom of ages.

"Are you girls just going to gawk or are we going to get on with the lesson?" asked Nani in annoyance breaking our reverie.

Nani indicated to a faded rug in the middle of the room. Varsha and I sat cross-legged on the rug, as Nani began.

"Today," she said, her voice a gentle melody, "we embark on a journey to understand the magic that flows in our veins."

Both Varsha & I were in our cotton nightdress & the floor felt cold but I ignored it. Varsha though was another story.

"Nani, can I go upstairs & put on a sweater?" she asked.

Nani growled in annoyance. "Stop complaining girl. Do you see me in my sweater? Look within then you will not feel the cold" she said as she used her flair for the dramatic to showcase her magic while at the same time teach us. She held out her hands, a subtle luminescence dancing between her fingertips.

"Magic, my dears, is not a force to be tamed, but a current to be embraced. Much like me"

Her smile held a touch of mischief, making us giggle in response. With a soft chant, Nani conjured a tiny orb of light that hovered above her hand. Its warm glow illuminated her face, lending her an otherworldly radiance.

"Magic is about connection," she explained, her words an invitation to a realm beyond the mundane. "A connection to the world around us and the depths within."

Varsha and I exchanged excited glances, our eagerness palpable. The orb also seemed to be emitting warmth & we no longer felt the cold. Nani beckoned us closer, and we formed a small circle. She placed her hands atop ours, the gesture communicating more than words could.

"Feel the energy that courses within you," she whispered, her touch like a conductor guiding a symphony of magic.

As we closed our eyes, Nani's voice wove a spell, guiding us to reach beyond the boundaries of our understanding. In the darkness behind my eyelids, colors danced, and a sense of weightlessness enveloped me. I felt a tingling sensation in my fingertips, like a whisper of wind brushing against my skin

"Imagine a small flame in your heart," Nani's voice was a soothing lullaby. "Let its warmth spread through your veins, connecting you to the very essence of magic."

A soft, flickering light materialized before my closed eyes, and I realized I wasn't alone in this journey. I was conscious of Varsha's presence which felt like a warm embrace as her energy entwined with mine- similar but a bit different. Just like how we were. Nani's words guided us through the delicate dance of magic. Nani asked us to summon a gentle gust of wind, to connect with the elements. As I felt it brush against my skin, a smile came unbidden to my lips. This felt good. This felt right. Nani's voice grew softer, like a fading echo.

"Remember, my dears, magic is an extension of yourself, a bond that intertwines your heart with the world's mysteries."

When I opened my eyes, Varsha's face mirrored my wonder. We shared a silent understanding—a new chapter had begun, and the magic that had long been confined to stories was now a tangible part of our lives.

Chapter 12 – Money & other matters

The next day morning when I came down for breakfast, Baba was at the dining table poring over a pile of documents with a furrowed brow. Usually, Baba was very composed and calm, a necessity in his profession. But today the breakfast dish forgotten, there was a mixture of exhaustion and frustration on his face. Seeing me he looked up & exclaimed

"Good morning, Veena. I was very tired last night but I wanted to speak with you. Something weird has happened at work. You will never guess who we are auditing this week" he said then without waiting for an answer he continued "It's your Mr. Khanna's firm. The tax audit... it's not going well." He sighed; his weariness apparent. "There are inconsistencies, inaccuracies... it seems they owe a substantial amount in taxes."

Baba, a Chartered Accountant with his own firm, loved the intricacies of numbers and financial puzzles. His firm was one of the most well-respected firms in Pune so it came as no surprise to me that the widow had asked my father to audit the taxes. What did surprise me was the timing at which this was being done. If my Baba had found discrepancies in taxes at first glance then I could only imagine the magnitude of the problems that lay ahead for the family. I asked the question foremost on my mind

"Wouldn't it make sense to put the audit on hold as the owner has passed away recently?" I asked curiously

"Ideally yes but in this case, his wife asked us to get things in order before the will is read & his assets are distributed" explained my father "Smart woman if you ask me. It is always better to get all money matters in order especially when a young man passes away- well relatively young in any case" he amended when I made a face.

"Moreover, his assets may get frozen if any of his clients are able to prove that he usurped money from them. Also in suspicious deaths, the assets may definitely be frozen if they suspect any of his legal heirs" Informed my father. He was well read in legal matters as well being a businessman himself.

"How much is his total worth Baba?" I asked outright wanting to know if there were any hidden assets my father had managed to find.

"Well Mr. Mehul Khanna may not have been a very nice human being but he sure is a rich one. I would estimate his total net worth to be around 200-250 Crore INR"

"Wow!" Varsha whistled as she entered the dining room "That is a lot! No wonder that chic was hitting on him"

"But how can he have so much just by practicing law even if he is murdering his clients? I think Vinay was right he must definitely be involved in gambling or drugs" I asked.

"That may well be the case" said Baba thoughtfully "But there is one more strange thing I found. Most of Mr. Khanna's assets are tied in properties he owns across various cities," said my father. "In fact, few of them would probably be ancestral properties & have been passed on to Mehul as inheritance. Though I have not seen any papers indicating the chain of inheritance- only the maintenance bills & the gift deeds"

"Strange!" I exclaimed "But if that is the case how come the properties are not in the name of his father but him? Also no one in Pune had heard of him or any of the Khanna's before his murder?" I asked "I mean no news ever in the papers or even the tabloids & his wife in spite of being an actress does not seem to mingle much with the who's who of Pune high society" I wondered aloud.

"It does seem strange but maybe he preferred it that way. After all the less people knew about what he owned the less the chances of them suing him," said Baba.

"I guess that makes sense though if Pinky married him for the lifestyle & she did not get a chance to flaunt it to her former friends by joining the high society life, she would be resenting him" I said thinking back to my interaction with the woman in question.

“Maybe they fell out of love for that reason & then Mehul started finding pleasure elsewhere,” said Varsha giving exaggerated winks.

Filing away this bit of information for later, I decided to tackle the wallpaper for the Poonawala’s that morning.

As I stepped into Mr. Pratik Rao's wallpaper store, I was amazed as usual at the beauty surrounding me. Mr. Rao was my go-to supplier, someone who had always delivered quality and innovation. Today's task was a bit different, though—a custom wallpaper design that held sentimental value. I knew I would have to use all tools in my arsenal to get what I wanted.

"Good morning, Mr. Rao," I greeted him with a smile. "I have a unique project in mind, and I'm hoping you can help me bring it to life."

As I explained Charmie and Mrs. Poonawala's request for a family tree illustration wallpaper, I could see the gears turning in Mr. Rao's mind. The challenge of creating a design that was both elegant and meaningful was evident in his expression.

"I'd love to take this project on," he said thoughtfully. "But Veena, you know custom designs like this usually take a bit longer, especially with the intricate details involved."

I understood his concern about timelines, but I also knew that Charmie and Mrs. Poonawala were eagerly waiting for this unique addition to their home & I couldn’t push the timeline for this. I leaned in a bit, my tone a mixture of assurance and promise.

"Mr. Rao, I completely understand your concern about the timeline," I began, my voice sincere. "But think about it—this custom design could open up a whole new avenue for your business. Elite clientele who not only appreciate the finer details but who are willing to pay a premium for something that's tailored to their tastes. Imagine the reputation you could build."

Mr. Rao's eyes brightened; his interest piqued by the prospect.

"And not just that," I continued, my voice gaining momentum. "You have my word that if this project goes smoothly and on time, I'll recommend your services to other clients in my network. Imagine the possibilities, Mr. Rao."

He nodded slowly, his scepticism giving way to a glimmer of excitement. As I spoke, I could see the wheels turning in Mr. Rao's mind. The promise of new horizons and increased profits seemed to outweigh his initial reservations.

"Alright, Veena," he finally said with a grin. "You've got yourself a deal. Let's create a masterpiece that not only enhances the Poonawalas' home but also takes my business to new heights."

I knew the power of a well-crafted argument & as we began discussing the design details, I couldn't help but feel a sense of satisfaction. Not only was I helping my clients, but I was also fostering opportunities for local businesses like Mr. Rao's to thrive. This was why I had entered this line of business after all. I left the shop with the design & colour scheme finalized as well as a committed delivery date. There was a spring in my step as Vinay & I were meeting for our date at a coffee shop.

The aroma of freshly brewed coffee welcomed us as Vinay and I stepped into the cozy coffee shop. It was a relatively new shop which had opened up in a by lane. Soft jazz music played in the background, creating a soothing ambiance. The lighting was dim casting a warm glow on the wooden tables. The menu offered a wide an array of coffee and dessert choices. We found a corner booth that offered a perfect vantage point of the street. Vinay's green eyes met mine, as we navigated the selection. Both of us opted for creamy cappuccinos while exchanging the mundane happenings of the past 2 days. Our coffee arrived shortly, the rich aroma mingling with the sweet scent of the pastries on display. As we sipped our drinks, we discussed topics ranging from politics to favourite books. I was amused to know that contrary to popular belief, Vinay actually preferred mystery to action while both of us were strong proponents of democracy. As the evening wore on, the coffee cups were replaced by dessert plates, and we indulged in sweet treats that perfectly complemented the rich coffee flavours. Vinay's smile was infectious, his presence a calming presence that made the worries of the day seem distant. However, as the time to leave approached, I reluctantly broached the topic of the case knowing it would intrude on our time together. But I knew I was probably on a clock if I wanted to save Mr. Khanna's soul.

"So, is it true that if a person is convicted of murder of another person, they cannot inherit the property of that person?" I asked Vinay. I was trying to keep the question generic but Vinay caught on.

"Why are you asking me this?" he asked.

I told him about my father's firm doing the tax audit for Mr. Khanna's widow & also about him having inherited a lot of his assets presumably from his grandparents or grand uncles.

"Do you think that this murder was committed for inheritance?" asked Vinay

"I heard some women talking during the funeral about a prenup & how Mrs. Pinky Khanna won't get a penny from the estate apparently. These were her film industry friends & they all seemed to be feeling sorry for her" I said "but wont the son inherit? Sanish, I mean. He & Maisha are the legal heirs of Mehul, right?" I continued

"You were quite busy at the funeral I see" said Vinay "To answer your question - If person is convicted then yes, he or she cannot inherit but only if the conviction is upheld. If they are proven innocent then they can definitely inherit." He continued. "Besides if it's not Mrs. Khanna then who is the benefactor of his will? I wonder. Maisha & Rahul are both minors & will need a legal guardian. Perhaps I should have a meeting with the firm handling Mr. Khanna's will. This case is proving to be more difficult than I initially anticipated," said Vinay

"May be Nemina will be able to help clear some things tomorrow" I said.

"I certainly hope so. A lot is riding on this case you know" continued Vinay "solving a high-profile murder like this will definitely give a boost to my career which is exactly what my father is expecting"

Listening to him, I couldn't help but feel a surge of empathy. The weight of the situation was palpable, the pressure of finding answers for a high-profile case like this must be immense. I couldn't help but appreciate his honesty in sharing his innermost thoughts with me. Once again, I felt as if our paths had crossed for a reason. My ability to interact with the supernatural world provided a perspective that was missing from the investigation. In order to unravel the truth behind Mr. Khanna's murder, I only needed Vinay to trust me as a partner & share his findings with me.

"And what does your mother expect" I asked to lighten his serious mood

"Oh! She expects me to find a nice girl, get married & settle down" said Vinay looking at me & winking which caused my heart to melt a little.

"Hmm... so promotion first followed by marriage right Mr. Detective"

"I think it may just go hand in hand. You see the girl I like loves mysteries" he smirked again as I blushed furiously.

With the night growing darker outside, we reluctantly realized that it was time to leave. As we stepped out of the coffee shop, the city lights shimmered like stars in the distance. Vinay's gaze met mine, and in that simple moment, I knew that the time to confide in him was drawing near. Every time we met, I had to take conscious efforts to not blurt out about my magic in front of him & it was becoming more & more difficult. I smiled back at Vinay feeling the weight of my guilt for not being honest with him. He gently gave me a peck on the cheek.

After coffee, I practically floated back to my office to pick up my design folders before heading home. But I was surprised to see Mrs. Pinky Khanna on my doorstep.

"Hello Veena, I had come to apologize for my behavior at the funeral & also to talk to you. Can we talk?" she asked.

"Sure, but I am about to head home. Let me just make a quick phone call" I said as I called Nani & explained that I would be delayed on account of Mrs. Khanna. Pinky smiled when I was done with my phone call.

"Your family is lucky that you keep them informed. At our house Maisha just comes & goes as she pleases" said Pinky with a frown.

I invited her into my office & asked her to get comfortable on the sofa as I kept the coffee for brewing.

"I am sorry for assuming that you were one of Mehul's little girlfriends. I should have realized you couldn't be one of those girls you are too pretty to be one" said Pinky as she took the first sip of coffee "And clearly too independent & intelligent as well" she continued looking around the office.

"I like your taste. Nothing in my house is as per my taste. Not even my own bedroom. All is done as per the choices of Maisha" she said with great distaste.

Mother & step daughter definitely had issues is what I could gather from Mrs. Khanna's complaining.

"Never mind. Now I will have my house designed as per my choice. Maybe you can help me with that? You are an interior designer, right?" she asked with a sweet smile.

Though it was too soon for Pinky to be thinking of renovating the house after the death of her husband, I found it strange that Maisha had so much say in the current design of Khanna Bungalow. Perhaps Mehul had spoiled the girl since she had no mother & that is the reason why she had no respect or empathy for anyone but herself.

It would explain her behavior with her grandfather to some extent. Giving my best fake smile I replied

"I would love to help you redesign your home. Perhaps we can keep just Maisha's room as per her tastes & change the rest of the house" I said tactfully.

"Oh, she decorates her own room. No designer is allowed to give inputs on her weird art prints or her choice of décor items. They look more like horror relics than antiques if you ask me" said Pinky wrinkling her nose. "Thankfully Mehul did not take all her inputs else I would have refused to live in the house" announced Pinky huffily.

We discussed a bit more on what I could do with the mansion that Pinky currently lived in. She also wanted to know if it was possible to put in a pool at the back & I informed her that I would have to survey the property in detail before giving her any plans & we would also have to get permissions. As we finished our coffee, she took my leave.

"Thank you for taking time out to speak with me. I felt guilty for pouncing on you that day. I will be in touch with you for the designing after a couple of months" She picked up her expensive purse & sashayed out of my office leaving me with even more questions.

Chapter 13 – Nemina

The next day arrived bright & early. Today was the day that Vinay & I were meeting Nemina. She had asked us to meet her in the afternoon at a little-known place for which she had shared the Google location. I had to check up my custom wall paper sample in the morning & approve the design & color shades post which Vinay would pick me up from my office & we would drive down to meet Nemina. That was the plan. I was also planning a visit to the garage later in the day. So currently I was perusing through my wardrobe trying to find something suitable for a site visit as well as a meeting with a suspect. Finally, I settled on wide leg jeans & a peasant top. It was casual enough for a meeting & practical enough for a site visit.

Just as I was about to start getting ready, Varsha barreled into my room yelling out

"Di, I need to borrow your red earrings".

"Why can't you wear your own earrings for once Varshu?" I asked tamping down my irritation.

"I have a date di." said Varsha making a face

"Who with?" me

"With Nakul."

"Who the hell is Nakul? Aren't you like in love with Harry?" I asked with my best mocking face.

"Di, Harry is the one I will eventually marry but don't I need to experiment with others first?"

Was she kidding me...?

"Experiment? This isn't science Varshu. What if this Nakul guy gets upset of you stringing him along?"

My curiosity got the better of me though I kept reminding myself that delving too deep into Varsha's life would just give me a headache.

"Stringing him along indeed! Where do you even learn these words Di? Do you like note down these phrases from old Hollywood movies just to bring them up in conversations with me? Next you will ask me if he is courting me!" Varsha replied with an incredulous expression on her face

"We are both doing TP Di! That is what people my age do! You won't understand. Just Chill!"

"Oh, whatever it's not like I am a decade older than you" I argued

"But you sure behave that way" said Varsha blowing a raspberry & dangling my rough-cut silver ruby danglers from her ears.

"You better not lose those Varsha. You know they are my favorite" I warned

"Don't worry Di. You will get them back as good as new" Varsha swayed out of the room just in time for me to see my new red sling bag dangling from her shoulder.

"Varsha, you come back & give me my bag right now!" I shouted after her

"Sorry Di, I am running late. Don't worry I will get this back with the earrings" the door slammed shut in the wake of my tornado of a sister.

I would have to keeping my accessories under lock & key to keep them from my sister I thought as I got ready. I was a little apprehensive whether the design I had conceptualized would translate as well on paper but I need not have worried. The custom wallpaper panel which Pratik showed me exuded an air of timeless elegance, a visual ode to heritage and lineage. The family tree was set against a backdrop of rich, velvety burgundy. The design capturing the essence of a bygone era, transporting observers to a world where tradition and luxury intermingle seamlessly. He explained to me that the heart of the wallpaper would be the meticulously illustrated family tree. The wallpaper would turn out exactly as I wanted it. Happy with a morning well spent, I headed to my office. Vinay met me there & we set out for the meeting.

The 'coffee shop 'that Nemina wanted a meeting in was more of a shanty or a chai ki tapri. It was nowhere near the city & was run by a young couple who I presumed knew Nemina personally. They also seemed to be expecting us. The man was working behind the counter at the tea station while the woman was at the cash register. The shanty had a thatched roof & wooden benches were placed around for the customers. There were electric lanterns hung on the walls at regular intervals along with some old tea ads which were framed. Someone had taken effort to make the place seem eclectic & homely. The cash register held glass jars filled with large cookies & packaged sweet buns. Unlike other shanties though this place was immaculately clean but weathered. The smell of cardamom filled the air as the tea boiled in a large pateli. We seemed to be the only 2 customers in the shanty at this time but that was possibly because we had come before tea-time. I was sure that is how Nemina had scheduled it. The woman at the cash counter smiled & introduced herself as Neetu & asked us if we were friends of Nemina. She indicated for us to occupy a bench at the very back of the shop.

When she came to take our orders, she started talking

"Nemina didi comes here for her evening tea every day. Such a nice girl she is & so responsible. Taking care of her younger brother at such a young age. Nimish is lucky to have her" she said.

"Do you know who we are" asked Vinay suspiciously

"Nemina only said that 2 of her friends would be joining her for her afternoon tea today. A handsome man with green eyes & a pretty lady. Since you two fit the description, I assumed you are the friends she mentioned. She is not in any trouble, is she?" asked Neetu fearfully.

"No ...no she is not in any trouble" I swiftly inserted.

"Vinay was just pulling your leg. He does that sometimes" I gave a stern look to Vinay.

It wouldn't do to spook the messenger if we wanted to meet Nemina. We ordered a plate of onion bhajia & 2 cups of cardamom or elaichi tea. After a few minutes a girl walked in & sat at our table. I could feel magic wafting off her & all my senses were immediately on the alert. She was wearing a simple salwar kurta & had covered her face partially with a dupatta with which she had demurely covered her head. I was about to ask her to relocate to another table when she took off the dupatta & revealed her face. Immediately she started talking.

"Hello, I am Nemina. I was at the 'Glocal Junction' with Mr. Khanna when he died. Do you remember me?" she asked looking directly at me.

I now looked at her more carefully. Without the makeup, the jewelry & the glamorous clothes, she was a plain girl. She was younger than I expected & not exceptionally pretty but it was definitely the same girl from the restaurant. The makeup had made her look older I realized. She would be about Varsha's age I estimated as I nodded in answer to her question. It was definitely Nemina.

"Yes. I remember you. You wanted to practically run away from the restaurant after what happened. Why have you called us here?" I asked getting straight to the point.

"I ...I wanted to talk to you but I didn't know who you were. I know you two are the only people who will believe me when I say that I had nothing to do with Mehul's murder" she declared as she looked at Vinay & gripped his hand.

As she moved closer, I could feel the magic flowing beneath her skin. I did not like the way she was touching Vinay. I glowered at her as she continued to make eyes at Vinay & suddenly as if stung her hand moved away from Vinay's. She looked at me in astonishment. She looked a bit frightened but Vinay seemed relieved as he gently extricated his hand & placed it on his knee.

"Why do you think we are the only 2 who will believe you?" he asked. She seemed a little taken aback that Vinay wouldn't just take her word for it. I believed she had use or was trying to use the same magic on Vinay which she had used on Inspector Aniket but for some reason Vinay was immune to it – interesting...

"Because I loved Mehul. I would never hurt him" she said earnestly once again trying to reach for Vinay's other hand when he placed his tea cup on the table.

This time I had had enough. I tilted Vinay's cup with magic such that the hot tea sloshed. The moment the hot tea made contact with her skin; she cried out.

"I am sorry. I am so...so sorry" Vinay was dabbing her hand with his handkerchief. He was embarrassed at his clumsiness not realizing my role in it.

"It's ok" she said looking directly at me "I won't try to touch you again"

Vinay was a bit confused by the exchange but did not push her as he too was clearly uncomfortable at the way she was throwing herself at him. I now knew why she had called me specifically to meet her. She had probably sensed my magic back at the restaurant itself & assumed that I too would have been able to see the red mist which she had seen. But that in no way proved her innocence to me. Meanwhile, Nemina had returned Vinay's handkerchief. She said she preferred to wipe her hand with her own handkerchief. As she took out her handkerchief, I noticed that it looked to be expensive with black hemming on the lacy borders & a small skull embroidered in a corner. The girl certainly had classy taste - outlandish but maybe it was the magic in her. After she had cleaned herself the best she could, she motioned to Neetu who brought her a cup of ginger tea. Nemina smiled at her & waited for her to leave the table before she started talking

"I met Mehul 6 months ago when he had come as a guest lecturer in our college. I was struggling & thinking of dropping out of college at that point in time. The couple who run this tea stall are my distant cousins on my mother's side. She passed away 2 years ago. Now it is only me & Nimish. My father is still around but he is a drunkard who doesn't care about us.

I was managing college & my brothers school expenses somehow by working part time at a local bakery. We had run out of savings & I had already sold all my mother's jewelry. Fortunately, my mother had hidden it before Papa could hock it & I was the only one who knew where. I also knew that once I got a degree, I would be able to get a decent job but with a year left, I was not sure if I would be able to manage the fees. I was just overwhelmed that day" her face took on a faraway look as if reliving the day

"That day they put my name on the defaulters list for students who hadn't paid their fees. I had only 15 days to pay & seeing my name on the list I burst into tears. That is how Mehul saw me. Before I realized I was pouring my heart out to him. He listened patiently & assured me things would work out. Had he offered to pay my fees, I would never have accepted" She looked at me with a determined look "I have my pride. I would have managed somehow but he offered me a job in his law firm as his assistant. The salary would comfortably allow me to pay my fees & my hours would still be part-time. You have to realize that no matter how it looked, Mehul was never inappropriate with me" Nemina said but she was averting her eyes.

"You mean he was willing to sponsor your education for essentially nothing in return?" I asked in disbelief.

"All he wanted was love" said Nemina

"The physical kind no doubt" said Vinay with a growl.

"What is so wrong in that?" asked Nemina defiantly "You think anyone else would have done what he did for a girl like me? Let's be real here. I now have a flat in my name in a good society & enough funds to complete my education. I don't regret what I did"

I could see that Nemina was more a victim of her circumstances. Vinay though was another story. Had Mehul been with us at that point, I was sure Vinay would have beaten him up for taking advantage of a young girl. I could practically see the vein in his forehead. I gently placed my hand over his soothing his temper with my magic. I was glad to see this side of him though. It showed me the kind of man he was – not just a detective but a decent human being as well.

"So, what were you doing in the restaurant that day?" I asked trying to get us back to the topic at hand.

"I had graduated with a first class that day. Mehul wanted the celebration to be grand so he asked me to choose a restaurant. I chose Glocal junction because I had seen it many a times but had never been able to afford a meal here" her eyes had taken on a faraway look. "The soft lighting, the aromas wafting out from the door & the people all dressed in their finest - all of it was very inviting. Mehul even let me order food of my choice without even checking the prices. But I don't think I was appropriately dressed for the place. The staff looked at me as if I didn't belong" Nemina's cheeks were flushed possibly remembering the mortification of that day. Then she brightened considerably

"But Mehul said I looked beautiful. I had worn the dress he had bought for me"

Vinay's hands were balled into fists at his sides & in spite of my hand resting on his arm he seemed to be fighting his baser instincts. I was not sure I felt any differently. The dress Nemina was wearing was meant for a hooker & was neither suitable nor appropriate for the place. Realizing that Vinay was having difficulty talking due to his anger, I prodded Nemina

"Then what happened?"

"Don't you know what happened?" challenged Nemina "Isn't that why you got up from your table & rushed to our table?" she was glaring at me.

Vinay was astounded at this turn of events. He was about to question me when Nemina's phone rang. Since she had placed it face up on the table, I could see the DP of the caller which was a young boy of about 13. He looked similar to Nemina. The brother I guessed.

"When are you coming home Didi? I am waiting for you to have my evening meal."

I could hear him through the mobile. The call transformed Nemina's face in seconds from a grumpy young woman to a loving sister. Talking in a soft voice she replied

"Hey Champ, I promise I'll be there soon to join you, but for now, don't let your food get cold. Go ahead and tuck in, and I'll catch up with you in no time. I have made your favourite oats recipe & it should still be warm in the casserole. Sorry champ but this is taking more time than I thought. If you wait for me, you will be late for school"

"Ok Didi. I will put the remaining food in the microwave for you. See you later alligator" Nimish said

"See you champ. Love you" replied Nemina.

The smile on her face vanished the moment she looked at me.

"Nemina, I know you don't know me & have no reason to trust me but I want the real murderer to be caught. I am not trying to implicate you. So can you please tell me what you saw?" I said in a calm voice. Vinay was a little confused as to where this was heading.

"Ok fine. There was a red mist which encircled us" said Nemina in a resigned tone

"Mehul started choking almost immediately" she said with a gloomy expression "I tried to protect him but it was over within seconds"

"Yes. That is also what I saw" I said & the relief on Nemina's face was palpable.

"I can't believe you kept this from me" Vinay was looking at me accusingly "You could have told me this the same day both of you or either of you. Veena you could have told me this at any point in time later too!"

"Would you have believed me Vinay" I asked looking cautiously at him.

"What is not to believe? This red mist must have been some sort of invisible poisonous gas which was only visible in close proximity," said Vinay.

"Poisonous gas???" Nemina looked at me incredulously.

"Yes, that is exactly what it must have been. There was a red gas that was released near their table probably by someone & that is what I had gotten up to investigate" I said before Nemina could speak.

"Hmm... strange that no one else remembers seeing any gas – even the staff didn't mention it. What I don't understand is how did it not affect you" he asked Nemina.

"Maybe it was a bio-weapon which was engineered specifically for Mehul's DNA" said Nemina looking at me.

"Wow! That seems like something out of a sci-fi movie but possible never the less" said Vinay as Nemina heaved a sigh of relief

"Let me call up the medical examiner & ask him to check for any unidentifiable gas poisoning" said Vinay excitedly stepping away from the table to make the call. As soon as Vinay was out of earshot, Nemina looked accusingly at me.

"You haven't told him who you are" said Nemina accusingly.

"Why should I?" I asked confused

"Well, isn't he like your boyfriend or something?" she asked

"No. We just met at the restaurant" I replied testily.

"So, you two aren't dating?" She asked with narrowed eyes her interest piqued

"We sure are – not that it's any of your business. Besides I don't think Vinay would be interested in college girls" I said with an irrational burst of jealousy.

"Whatever you need to tell yourself. I am not interested in your man though the packaging is quite nice" said Nemina with a wicked glint in her eyes as she eyed Vinay appreciatively.

"What exactly are you? I can sense that you are powerful but you are not a witch. Yet you definitely wield magic" she asked

"So, you are a witch, is it?" I asked avoiding her question.

"Yes, I am a witch. Same as my mother just not as powerful" said Nemina defiantly. "But what are you" she asked again.

"I... I'm just an ordinary girl," I replied trying to dodge the question

"Really you want to play this game? Ordinary souls do not emit such enchanting vibrations. Your aura; it whispers of ancient magic. You are definitely not ordinary" said Nemina

"Fine! I am a Rakshasi & I think it would be prudent for you to not eye my guy!" I said in warning tone

"I am not afraid of you Rakshasi but perhaps you should be afraid of what's out there!" she spat

"Do you know anyone who might have wanted Mehul dead? Do you know who did this? Or is this just a fishing expedition to find what we know?" I asked

"I have my suspicions but nothing concrete... yet. I know magic was used to kill him though" she said

"Why didn't you try to protect him?" I asked curious to know the extent of her involvement.

"I did. I tried my level best to protect him with what little power & knowledge I have. You have to understand though- my mother passed away before she could teach me about my lineage"

"Yeah, we have that in common" I said feeling a sudden kinship with this girl

Nemina looked at me with surprise in her eyes. "You are lucky you have family then. All I have- had was Mehul. I had given him a protection symbol"

I remembered the tattoo I had seen & concluded that she could be telling the truth but I also knew that Nemina was a victim & she had magic at her disposal so how much could I really trust her?

"I think it will help you to follow the money trail" she said continuing.

"You know people keep mentioning that. Do you also think Mehul was killed for his money?" I asked but before Nemina could answer, I noticed Vinay returning back to the table.

"We need to stick to the poison gas story for now though you & I both know it was magic" I cautioned Nemina.

"Well, we can't really convince people that magic exists" said Nemina just as Vinay returned. He seemed to be excited.

"Thank you for sharing this with us. If you can think of anything more then don't hesitate to reach out to us" Vinay said earnestly as he took his seat & handed her his card.

She plugged his number into her mobile & put the card in her purse. Then looking at Vinay she said-

"I am going to head home now. My brother as you know is waiting. But I think the answers you are looking for may be too much for you detective"

I knew that her cryptic would message only made Vinay more determined to find the murderer.

"I feel sorry for her" said Vinay after Nemina had left.

I did not know what to make of the meeting. While it did not feel like Nemina was lying, the fact that she was a witch & was with Mehul when he died meant she was at the top of my suspect list. Her information was also somewhat vague but I decided to ask my father about it never the less. As I saw Nemina's retreating back, an inexplicable feeling gripped me. All my instincts were urging me to follow Nemina. I made an excuse to Vinay saying I had needed to use the restroom. He seemed doubtful considering the place we were at - but I told him I would find someplace nearby & almost ran out of the shop before he could ask me any more questions.

My assumption was that Nemina would be staying somewhere nearby since she had chosen this location. Fortunately, I saw her on the other side of the road hurrying in a direction opposite to the one which we had come from. I put on my sunglasses & started following her. With careful steps, I trailed her from a distance. She moved with a purpose, unaware of my presence, her movements fluid and graceful.

I was careful to maintain a discreet distance, hiding behind trees or vehicles should she happen to glance back. All my senses were on high alert, as she turned a corner, my pulse quickened. A society of charming row houses emerged ahead, each had its own unique facade and an air of quiet elegance. So, this was the neighborhood that Nemina craved I thought to myself. It would offer her the kind of security needed for a young woman living alone with a child. The neighborhood was decent but not affluent. As she drew closer to a particular door, she paused & took out a bunch of keys from her purse. When Nemina disappeared behind the door, I seized the moment, committing the number of the row house to memory. I reached for a small notebook in my bag & jotted down the number. This was a clue, but where did this piece fit in the bigger puzzle - that was the question.

I then hurried back to the tapri lest Vinay get suspicious.

"Are you alright?" Vinay asked looking concerned as I entered the shop "I was about to go look for you."

I felt guilty lying to him but there was no way I could share my suspicions regarding Nemina & her magic without coming across as a lunatic

"I am fine. I just needed to pee very badly" I said.

I don't think Vinay was satisfied with my explanation but he didn't push. I couldn't explain more without going into the magic bit & I didn't think Vinay was ready to accept the truth yet. I would have to wait.

"So, what do you think" Vinay asked me as I took my seat.

"I think she is not as innocent as she would have us believe. I think she specifically called us here to showcase her vulnerable side to you. After all you are the lead investigator & she may have assumed that her helpless female routine would probably cause you to remove her name from the suspect list" I said teasingly.

Vinay turned thoughtful "Hmm... she has been taken advantage of that is for sure"

I hesitated at his response. "I do agree to that but isn't it possible that murdering her tormentor is her way of getting back? After all she now has everything, she needed from him. Maybe he was not willing to let her go" I voiced my opinion.

"May be but I keep coming back to the question - why did she insist that you accompany me? That doesn't make sense in the scenario you painted"

"Unless she thought you wouldn't take her word for the red mist story that she told us about. I think she needed me there to corroborate her" I hurriedly inserted. I needed Vinay to concentrate on the mist rather than the reason for my presence.

"You are right. I am still not fully convinced of her innocence. I will ask Aniket to put someone to track her movements".

Post the meeting with Nemina, Vinay came to drop me back home. As I was about to head inside, Mrs. Joshi accosted Vinay.

"So, I heard that you are the chief investigating officer for the murder in restaurant of that lawyer- Mr Khanna" she began. Then she looked at me "Why didn't you tell me that Mr. Vinay Verma here is with the police Veena? We have a detective in our midst visiting you regularly" she said with a sly smile

"No thief will dare enter the society now. Anyway, what I wanted to know Vinay – can I call you that?" she continued without giving him a chance to answer "It has been almost 2 weeks now. Do you know how he died? There has been nothing in the news. Was the food poisoned or did he get a heart attack or some other disease? You know my nephew & I often go to that restaurant – Glocal Junction. Apparently, this Mr. Khanna was foaming at the mouth is what I have heard"

Vinay was flabbergasted at being questioned like this in the middle of the road by an old lady. He was looking at Mrs. Joshi as if she had sprouted horns.

"Ma'am" he began "Oh! Don't call me Ma'am again. Have you forgotten? I am Hemlata... Mrs. Hemlata Joshi, Veena's neighbor; almost like a distant Aunt" she said looking at me.

"Umm... yes, I do remember you Mrs. Joshi. How can I forget you?" said Vinay as Mrs. Joshi positively preened at the presumed compliment.

"Mrs. Joshi" he continued "we don't have the liberty of releasing information to the public but you can be rest assured that it was not the food that killed Mr. Khanna. Glocal junction is off the hook" he smiled.

"Well, that is indeed good to know. You know it is one of my favorite restaurants. It is good to have friends in the police. Now that you are friends with Veena, I am sure I will get all information regarding crime in our area. At my age you can never be too careful. Thank you, inspector," she said

"Actually, its detective" Vinay said to her retreating back but she did not respond.

"That old lady is something" said Vinay as he smiled at me.

"Try living next to her" I commented waving him goodbye as I walked inside the bungalow.

Varsha was munching on a bag of chips & binging on Harry potter when I walked in.

"How was the meeting Di?" she asked pausing the movie. Varsha almost never paused her Harry potter marathon so she was definitely interested. Sitting down next to Varsha, I grabbed a chip from her bag.

"Hey! Get your own packet of chips. This one is mine" said Varsha yanking away the packet.

"Fine then I won't tell you what happened" I teased.

"Cmon di you tell me everything. Here you can have 2 chips & that's it" said Varsha extending the bag.

I took a deep breath, gathering my thoughts before speaking.

"Varsha, remember what I told you about that woman I met at the restaurant, Nemina?"

"She's magical isnt she?" asked Varsha.

I hesitated for a moment, choosing my words carefully.

"Yes Varsha, Nemina is... a witch."

A spark of surprise flickered in Varsha's eyes, and she leaned in closer, her curiosity piqued.

"A witch? Like, with magic and spells? The ones that fly on brooms? That kind? ... that is probably the reason for the tunnel vision, eh?"

"Yes, I suppose so" I replied.

Varsha's brows furrowed, her expression a mix of fascination and uncertainty.

"But how do you know she's a witch? Did she tell you?"

"Yes. She admitted it herself & then asked me what I was" I replied.

"You didn't tell her that did you?" asked Varsha incredulously

"She already knew I was magical Varsha there was no point hiding it. Besides I think she has been snooping around our house. Mrs. Joshi mentioned seeing her" I elaborated.

Varsha was out of her seat on the couch & excitedly grabbed my hand.

"That means she is your murderer Di. You should instruct your boyfriend to arrest her" she continued hopping up & down.

"Do you have her photo?" she asked grabbing my mobile.

"Calm down Varshu. Yes. I did click a photo when she was not looking" I said showing her the photo.

"And will you all please stop assuming that Vinay is my boyfriend!" I continued irritated

"This girl looks pretty ordinary nothing like a witch – neither ugly nor pretty" said Varsha as she handed me back my phone "Now what do you mean by 'you all'? Who else other than me said he is your boyfriend" asked Varsha narrowing her eyes.

"Nemina also seemed to think the same when she admitted that she is a witch" I said

"She has a better sense than you that's for sure. Did she also admit to the murder" asked Varsha.

I was quite irritated with my sister but there was no one else to discuss the magic stuff with available at that time so I answered

"No. She said she cared for Mehul but she did mention seeing the red mist"

"Care for him footing her bills you mean! Di, chances of there being 2 different magical creatures in this case are slim to none. I say arrest the witch"

"And charge her with what Varsha? We have no evidence. I cannot "instruct" Vinay to arrest her"

I said putting quotes on the word instruct & using my best sarcastic tone.

"Hey no need to get angry with me. What did you tell Vinay then?" asked Varsha

"Oh, we told him that both of us saw a red mist & he assumed that it was a poisonous gas or a bio weapon" I said guiltily

"A targeted bio weapon" said Varsha "Wow Di, you have got to tell him the truth"

"And have him think I am insane? Thanks, but no thanks. How are things with Harry?" I asked hoping to change the subject

"Nothing is happening with him Di. He has just broken up with his girlfriend. I have to wait at least a week to ask him out" asked Varsha with a fake sense of righteousness

"So next week then?" I asked

"You bet. I don't want any other girl to ask him out before I do" she said smirking.

"Btw this Nemina also has a kid brother" I said.

"Did you meet him as well?" asked Varsha.

"No but I do know where they stay" I grinned.

"You followed her, didn't you? Way to go Di. You would have made a fabulous detective" Varsha high-fived me "Just promise me you will be careful" she added as I nodded in response. Just then Nani called out to us as she entered the house possibly back from a walk.

"Girls I think it's time for another lesson"

Chapter 14 – Family dinner

As we gathered in the basement, Varsha & I were again whispering in anticipation of what the lesson entailed. Nani gave us a firm look as stood before us. As we ceased talking, her eyes sparkled with a mix of mischief and excitement.

"Today, my dears, we delve deeper into the realms of magic," she began, her voice teasing. Abruptly she used her fingers to zing both of us.

"Ouch" both Varsha & I yelled in unison as Nani laughed.

"Keep sharp girls. Magic won't teach you that. But today we shall learn to create a protective cocoon—a shield that will surround you, keeping you safe from harm and negative energies. Veena, you can use it the next time you encounter the witch. I wouldn't have been able to zing you had you thrown a shield. My magic would have rebounded from the shield. Let's start".

Varsha and I exchanged annoyed glances

"The demonstration was uncalled for" complained Varsha.

"C'mon now, how am I supposed to get my fun?" asked Nani with an amused smile.

Since Baba was going to be late, Nani had decided to schedule our second lesson earlier in the evening. This time too, we sat cross legged on the rug, our hearts racing with awe. Nani guided us through the steps, her words a gentle cadence that flowed like a melody. With each instruction, she painted a vivid picture in our minds, guiding us to visualize the cocoon taking shape around us.

"Imagine the cocoon, a shimmering barrier of energy, emanating from your very core. Feel its warmth, its strength, as it envelops you."

Closing my eyes, I focused on Nani's guidance, allowing my imagination to take flight. In my mind's eye, I saw the cocoon forming—a delicate lattice of light that expanded and solidified around me. The sensation was surreal, as if a veil of magic had draped itself over my being. Nani's voice continued to weave its magic, guiding us through the process of infusing the cocoon with our intentions.

"Pour your intent into the cocoon, let it become a reflection of your inner strength and purpose. Trust in the power that lies within you."

As I concentrated, a sense of empowerment surged through me. The cocoon felt like an extension of myself, a manifestation of my will and determination. I could almost feel the energy coursing through my veins, connecting me to the unseen currents of the universe. Nani's words reached a crescendo, and with a final flourish, she instructed us to seal the cocoon with a gesture of our choice. I raised my hands, palms facing outward, feeling a surge of energy flow from my fingertips, completing the enchantment.

Opening my eyes, I beheld the sight before me—a soft, iridescent cocoon of light encasing both Varsha and me. Nani immediately released 2 bolts of magic like before but now they rebound harmlessly from the cocoon back towards Nani who deflected them with minimal effort. Nani's smile was one of pride and joy,

"And that is how it's done" she said. "This protective cocoon is a symbol of your connection to the magical realm, a shield that reflects your inner strength. Remember, magic is not just about power—it's about intention, love, and the harmony between yourself and the universe."

As the cocoon dissipated, fading into the ether, I felt a sense of accomplishment wash over me.

The magic lesson had left Varsha & me exhausted. I slipped into a deep sleep almost immediately after dinner. My dreams were more vivid & some of them echoed with the laughter of my mother. However, I was unable to recall most of it as the first light of dawn filtered into my room.

Today was the day Vinay was coming over for dinner. The cook was not coming in for the morning as she had a wedding to attend but she had promised to be there on time for dinner to cook for 'our special guest' as Nani had whispered to her. Since my Nani refused to step into the kitchen, the task of making the breakfast fell to me & Baba. We decided to try our hand at Poha which is what I had seen Ma make many a times. My mother was a fantastic cook. Next to her job as a teacher the thing she enjoyed the most was cooking. Baba measured the poha & started soaking them in water while I was given the task of cutting the potatoes which would go into it. Kanda- batata poha with lots of dhania, wet coconut & lemon for flavor was a favorite of my father. However, on opening the fridge I realized that we only had one tiny twig of dhania left. Knowing that Baba would be disappointed without the dhania, I decided to try my hand at a spell Ma had taught me as a child. It was a simple enough spell to make the dhania sprig grow till it was enough for the meal.

Baba was busy chopping the onions so I washed the twig & placed it on the kitchen counter near the chopped potatoes. Then I started chanting the spell. At first nothing happened. Then slowly I could see the twig starting to grow. From 6 inches, it grew to 8 inches & then 12 inches. Then it sprouted a branch. I had stopped chanting hoping that it would stop growing now but the twig kept growing. It was now 2 feet & creeping out the kitchen window near the platform. I started panicking when I realized Mrs. Joshi was at her kitchen window & was looking in shock at what was happening.

"Veena, are you done? The tadka is ready" Baba was asking.

When I didn't answer he turned around from the gas & saw what was happening. For a moment I saw sheer terror reflected on his face but he quickly masked that then uttered a counter spell & clapped twice. The twig immediately stopped growing. Then he clapped some more & before I could realize what was happening, he had stepped out of the house. From the kitchen window I could see him talking to Mrs. Joshi from across the fence. She smiled & waved to me. Then seemingly satisfied with the outcome, Baba came inside the kitchen. Now, he was furious.

"What is it with you & magic? Can't you cook a simple meal without using a spell? This is all because of your Nani!" He fumed

"Get out right now. I will make the breakfast myself"

I had never seen Baba this angry

"I am sorry Baba" I said in a small voice. "I know you like dhania in your poha & there was almost none left. I thought I could do this simple spell that Ma had taught me to make the small twig we had grow, so that we would have enough. But I guess I forgot the incantation at the end to make it stop" I said looking at my Baba with tears in my eyes.

Seeing me, all the anger seemed to have left his body

"Yes, Swati loved to use that spell. She always teased me that she was saving loads of money by making things grow at home"

Baba had a wistful look on his face.

"I have heard her use the spell so many times I remembered the incantation to stop. Else it would never have stopped growing"

Baba took both my hands in his hands & looked pleadingly at me.

"Veena, you have got to promise me that you will stop using magic. Please promise it to me right now"

I didn't know what to do

"Tell me what happened to Ma, Baba. All these years you have been avoiding giving me answers. If she was in an accident, why did we never get the body? Why do you hate magic so much though you loved it when she performed magic?"

Baba looked at me in wonder

"I remember it Baba. Varsha may have been too young but I remember the way Ma used to put on little performances with her magic. She loved doing it for her school annual functions as well & you never had a problem with it then so why now?"

Baba avoided looking at me

"I cannot answer your questions beta. Some questions are better left unanswered but please you have to promise me stop using magic" he urged once again

" Magic is the last part of her I have" I said with tears in my eyes "I am sorry I cannot make that promise Baba" I said as I left the kitchen.

Having witnessed the wonder of magic & the extent to which it could affect the world we dwelled in; I believed I had no choice but to be well versed in the craft. I needed to be able to protect my family if the occasion ever arose. That was the best outcome for everyone concerned & I hoped my father would be able to see that one day. I left the house without my breakfast too emotionally wrung out.

I grabbed a vada-pav on the way. I was meeting Prakash at my office to discuss on the garage conversion project. Prakash was already waiting for me when I reached the office. I made 2 cups of cappuccino & we sat down for our first brain storming session. This was the most exciting part of any project for me. I had taken enough photos of the site which were now scattered all over my desk.

"Prakash, I am really excited about this conversion. Check out these photos" I had clicked basic photos of the site & mapped the measurements on the photos before taking the prints. "As I told you, they want to convert their garage into an apartment for a family. It's an old stone structure & as you know I love that style of construction. It was so cool even in the middle of the afternoon. This will definitely be different as we will be restoring something so old & giving it a new purpose" I said with a smile.

Prakash scratched his chin thoughtfully. I knew that it was not in his nature to give an exuberant reaction at the beginning of any project. While I was always the more excitable one, his experience with old sites & the practicalities of constructing or specifically restoring something had its own set of challenges. I expected him to be a bit critical.

"It definitely sounds interesting, Veena. What are we looking at in terms of layout and design?" he asked

"Well, the Gupta's garage has a decent amount of space, so we can definitely create a comfortable living area. I'm thinking an open-concept living room and kitchen, a bedroom, and a bathroom. We need to make sure it feels cozy but not cramped." I enthused

Prakash nodded in agreement.

"Got it. How about the utilities? Plumbing, electrical, heating?" he asked

"They're planning to keep it separate from the main house, so we'll need to set up new connections for water, electricity, and heating. I want to make sure they have all the modern amenities they need."

Prakash jotted down some notes.

"And what's the style we're going for? Any specific theme or colour scheme?"

"The Guptas mentioned they like a modern yet comfortable vibe. I'm thinking neutral tones with pops of colour, and some sleek furniture. We want to maximize the space without it feeling cluttered. However, I do not want to mess with the aesthetic of the structure from the outside so a cute stone cottage vibe would be perfect" I could almost visualize the finished project in my mind's eye

"Sounds good. And what about the windows and natural light?" asked Prakash jotting down more details while studying the photos.

"I noticed there's a good amount of natural light in the garage, so I want to make the most of it. But to entice families I am going to suggest adding a floor. They definitely have FSI & with more space the Guptas can also explore the option of Air BnB. We'll definitely need to add some new windows and maybe a sliding glass door for access to the backyard."

Prakash nodded; his pencil busy on the paper. "Great. And the timeline for this project?"

"That is the tricky part. The Guptas are hoping to have it done within a few months, so we need to work efficiently since we cannot let this delay the Poonawala project. Let's aim for a detailed design proposal within the next week."

At this time, I looked apprehensively at Prakash. While I hadn't committed to this timeline, my gut feeling was that if we asked for longer, the project would go to someone else. But Prakash flashed a confident smile & I heaved a sigh of relief.

"No problem, Veena. I'll start working on the estimates and logistics. The Poonawala site is almost ready & now that I know the wallpaper will be delivered on time, I am not worried. Looks like we have another exciting project on our hands."

"Absolutely, Prakash. I'm looking forward to transforming that garage into a cozy and functional apartment for the Guptas. Let's make it happen!"

Post my meeting, I spent the rest of the day answering emails & making more sketches for the garage conversion. Today was the day Vinay was coming down for dinner & I wanted to reach home early to get ready. I had also promised to help the cook Laxmi tai with the dinner prep. I left at precisely 5pm giving me plenty of time to get ready.

As usual, Vinay arrived at exactly 7pm. His sense of time was impeccable & was probably going to cause a few tiffs if he expected me to follow the same. While I was by no means tardy for this would not do in my line of work, for my personal commitments I always kept a buffer of 5-10 mins for myself. The dinner table was already set & the aroma of home-cooked food wafted through the air. Vinay seemed a bit awkward as he greeted everyone. His handshake with my father very stiff & formal. But gradually everyone seemed to relax as my father asked Vinay about his day & there was small talk about the weather (it had rained today marking the beginning of the monsoons).

Soon the discussion turned to Mr. Khanna's case & Vinay's investigation.

"So how many suspects do you have at this point in time Vinay?" Nani asked

"At this point in time there are too many people who had reasons to kill Mehul for me to consider them all as suspects" replied Vinay with a smile. I understood that he didn't want to divulge information.

"Vinay," she began with a sly grin "Wouldn't it be great if you could gleam the guilt of a person with magic"

Vinay's grin matched hers as he responded, "Well, Mrs. Desai, I'm a detective. I deal in facts and evidence. But I'm open to discovering whether the universe has some magic up its sleeve."

Varsha's eyes sparkled with mischief as she leaned in, "Ah, the quest for truth! I like that. Does that mean that you believe in true love or soul mates"

Vinay blushed- yes, he actually blushed at my little sister's inane question. Nani though wasted no time in steering the conversation back toward magic.

"Mr. Verma," she began with a sly grin, "am I to believe that are you are believer in the mystical?"

Vinay seemed lost in thought then replied

"Mrs. Desai, I am a student of science. It is my belief that whatever science cannot explain today, it will tomorrow. There is a logic behind everything that happens- even magic" said Vinay with a smile.

Nani frowned "You don't believe in a higher power? You don't believe in miracles? Can science explain how a frail woman who barely has enough strength to do her daily chores can protect her child from a leopard? Or how a man who has been plagued by cancer & has days to live makes a complete recovery overnight?"

"Mrs. Desai attributing everything that cannot be easily explained to magic is a dangerous way to live don't you think?" said Vinay with a challenge

"And not believing in magic is a totally morose way to live - don't you think Vinay?" said Nani almost jabbing Vinay with her finger.

My Nani always gave back as good as she got but I was apprehensive that things were getting a bit out of hand. I was about to interject when Baba, seeing this as an opportunity to push his own agenda chimed in,

"You see, Vinay, in the real world, we don't need magic to get things done. It's all about practical solutions."

Vinay's eyebrow arched in question to this response. He was slowly coming to terms with our family dynamics and it was clear he would get to witness them firsthand today.

"True, Mr. Pradeshi, but imagine if we could make traffic disappear with a wave of a wand?"

Varsha, always one to add her two cents, giggled,

"Or if we could magically get our homework done!"

Vinay laughed, playing along.

"Now that would be a useful spell!"

I was a bit relieved to see that Vinay could hold his own in a conversation with my father & my Nani. It was an impressive feat in my book to manage that without losing your mind or lashing out. He was neither intimidated nor shy of stating his own opinion. It was clear that he did not wish to alienate my father or my Nani & so far, he was managing to stay on the good side of both & doing a wonderful job of it. To prevent any further escalations, I decided to play mediator between the two contrasting viewpoints.

"Okay, okay, let's not turn this into a magical duel. Magic and practicality can coexist, can't they?"

Nani nodded, a twinkle of mischief still in her eyes.

"Of course, dear. After all, a little bit of magic adds flavour to life."

Varsha chimed in, winking at Vinay.

"See, Vinay, you're missing out on all the fun!"

Vinay chuckled, raising his hands in mock surrender. "You might be onto something, Varsha."

The rest of the dinner conversation veered towards safer topics like my work & the history of our house & everyone seemed to be having a good time. As the evening winded down, Vinay's warm smile held a touch of gratitude as he stood up, ready to say his goodbyes.

"Thank you, Mrs Desai & Mr. Pradeshi, for inviting me and for this delicious dinner," he said, his eyes flickering with sincerity.

Baba returned his smile, "You're welcome, Vinay. It was great having you here."

While Nani said "You better bring something other than those Malai sandwiches the next time you come. A bottle of whisky would be nice"

Baba & Vinay both looked at her with their mouths hanging open

"Oh! Don't be so shocked. Can't old ladies enjoy their drinks?" Vinay burst out laughing

"Don't worry Mrs. Desai I will be sure to carry a bottle of Jack Daniel's the next time I come"

As our eyes met, across the table, there was genuine amusement in his eyes. I went to outside to say goodbye to Vinay. The air between us felt charged with a connection that had been growing stronger. As I looked into Vinay's eyes, I leaned in with a sense of anticipation, my heart skipping a beat as I felt his presence draw closer. But just as our lips were about to meet, a playful voice cut through the moment.

"Hey, you two! Mrs Joshi is checking out the action through the window. Do you want to give her a show?"

Varsha's voice, both amused and teasing, broke our near-kiss, and I couldn't help but laugh, my cheeks flushing with a mix of embarrassment and amusement. Vinay joined in the laughter, his eyes twinkling as he stepped back.

Varsha, grinning mischievously, continued, "I'm heading to bed. Though you guys should continue your romantic rendezvous without an audience! May be the garden behind the house" she gave Vinay a wink.

Vinay chuckled; his playful spirit evident. "Maybe next time, Varsha."

As Varsha disappeared inside, leaving us in an amusingly awkward aftermath, I met Vinay's gaze once again. The moment had been both endearing and slightly comical.

"Looks like we'll need to find a more opportune moment for that kiss," Vinay said, his tone light.

I grinned, nodding in agreement. "Definitely. I guess we'll just have to wait for the stars to align."

Vinay nodded. He looked into my eyes & said "Veena, your family is great. Even though you guys don't see eye to eye it is quite clear that you are very close to each other. I thoroughly enjoyed meeting all of them."

As Vinay waved goodbye with a final smile, I couldn't help but feel our connection had strengthened. With our paths intertwined in both serious moments and light-hearted ones, I realized that regardless of what happened next, Vinay was becoming more special to me each day one shared meal, one shared laugh and one near-kiss at a time.

Chapter 15 – The attack

The next day morning I had my second visit to the garage of Mr. & Mrs. Gupta. The structure itself was built to house either 3 big cars or multiple 2 wheelers. I was sure it was initially visualized as more of an outhouse for the help rather than a garage since the structure was quite old. The Guptas themselves possessed 1 car which was parked on the other side of the bungalow. The car was seldom used & since both of them had retired from prestigious positions - him as a high paying V.P & her as a college professor, they were mainly looking for company by renting out this unit to a family. I had told them in the first visit itself that to entice a family they would have to expand the space- build a floor on top of the existing structure, build some internal walls & possibly a small garden. They had mostly agreed to the plans but the FSI of the property needed to be checked. I didn't foresee a problem in that as the plot size was large. The existing bungalow had a big garden at the back & lots of empty space. If done right, this project could also become a very profitable Air BnB. Mrs. Gupta came to greet me & hung out while I was measuring the space & clicking more photos. The designing software I was working with would give better 3D visualizations with more photos. Once I had what I needed, Mrs. Shalini Gupta invited me in for tea.

Mrs. Gupta was a stern lady. She would have been the one professor the parents would have trusted to get their kids back on track. In her retirement too she had maintained the same demeanor & hence did not deem it suitable to talk to me whilst I worked. Now though she was in a chatty mood. Today she was wearing a handloom silk saree which seemed to be her signature style. She poured 2 cups of tea & laid out some cookies she had baked herself.

"These are delicious"

I complimented taking a bite of the oats & raisins cookie. I hadn't had anything to eat since morning after a toast & a cup of coffee as I had to get to the garage early. The cookie melted in my mouth & I sighed in contentment at its buttery texture. Mrs. Gupta seemed delighted with my reaction. She urged me to take more cookies. It was apparent that she was an accomplished baker.

"My daughter loves these chocolate chip ones" she said taking one herself "I send 2 boxes of cookies to her every month"

The Guptas had one daughter who stayed in Pune itself. She worked in IT & had recently gotten married. Her job required a lot of travel. There were photos of her displayed prominently all over the house. It was clear from Mrs. Gupta's talk that mother & daughter were quite close & I suddenly felt a pang of envy & unexpected sorrow to never have had that kind of bond with my own mother while growing up. As I tried to get my emotions under control, I noticed that my hands were glowing. I hid them in the pockets of the kurti before Mrs. Gupta could notice. She was narrating an incident from her daughter's business trip & I could tell she was quite proud of her daughter. When she finished, I asked to be excused to use the restroom to compose myself. After splashing some water on my face & getting my emotions under control, I was able to stop the glow. I now understood what my Nani had been telling me about our magic being connected to our emotions. I recalled the other times this had happened in school- girls tripping on seemingly nothing if they teased me or boys blabbering embarrassing secrets about themselves if they said anything bad about my family. Varsha & I had been subjected to our share of teasing thanks to my Nani.

Unlike others in her age groups, my Nani - Nalini Desai was not like a 'normal' grandmother. For starters she was not scared of technology. She had embraced it wholeheartedly though selectively as the magic of the modern world which was accessible to all. Because of her lineage her health was robust & her mind was still sharp. Her preferred outfit was long flowy kaftans which had now come back in fashion but were very unusual 15 years ago. She recited mantras with bizarre intonations & worshipped the 5 elements. Her creation of illusions was legendary & many a times when we were children bored at home in school vacations, she had kept us entertained with illusions of grand castles or of terrible beasts to be fought. In hindsight though I realized that those kids had probably all gotten some form of weird punishments. Girls ended up getting upper lip hair which resembled moustaches or kept losing their stationery items while boys got severe upset stomachs. Slowly they all realized to stay away from Varsha & me. As a result, we did not have a lot of close friends. I never minded that for I was absolutely fine hanging out with my little sister. Varsha though longed for company & now in college with a fresh set of people, she seemed to have found her own clique of friends. As all these memories came flooding back, I got my first real feel of what Nani had said about power.

When I came back to the living area, Shalini ji was going through some of my sketches in my sketch book. She looked up guiltily sensing my presence.

"Sorry beta. I couldn't help myself. I hope you don't mind?" she asked.

"No Mrs. Gupta. I am glad to know that you are interested & as invested in this as I am" I replied with a smile.

"Well good then. Can you show me the software that you use?" she asked with the curiosity of a child.

Since Mrs. Gupta seemed very interested in the whole design process. I gave her a basic demo of the software I used. She asked me some questions & really liked what I had planned for their space. The conversation veered to Mr. Gupta & Shaliniji told me that her husband was thinking of starting consulting services as sitting at home was driving him crazy. They were planning to use part of the area in the main bungalow as an office with a separate entrance. She added that they might need my help in designing that as well. After discussing on the designs, Mrs. Gupta who was staring out of the window remarked

"Have you heard about the unfortunate business with the Khanna's? They moved here some years back though I don't know them that well"

When I saw the window through which Mrs. Gupta was staring at, I noticed that the Khanna's bungalow was visible on the horizon.

"Pinky that's Mrs. Khanna does take extra efforts to be a good neighbor. She had come for a visit with some flowering shrubs when they moved in as some of the other neighbors had informed her that I liked gardening. I offered her these cookies & she also loved them," said Mrs. Gupta.

"She had asked me if I could teach her to bake but I told her I didn't have time since I was working then. May be now I can start the class." She continued.

"Anyway, some days back I heard that Pinky's her husband had passed away. The police seem to think it was a murder. I tend to believe it may have been a heart attack. That is their bungalow" said Mrs. Gupta as she pointed out the Khanna's bungalow to me.

I noticed that only a part of the garden of the Khanna mansion was clearly visible from the window of Mrs. Gupta's house. I could see the gardener pruning some shrubs there.

"I had been to their house for the funeral" I said.

"Do you know the Khanna's Veena?" asked the surprised Mrs. Gupta. I told her about my connection with the murder & the reason why the police suspected that it was murder.

"Hmm... no wonder my husband didn't like the Khanna's. Good riddance for Pinky if you ask me. He was cheating on her with a new woman every month. The poor girl! My husband had told me to keep my distance from Pinky but I think I can make up my own mind on such matters, isn't it?" she asked.

I smiled in amusement.

"Well, I hope they find the murderer. At least that way the widow & his children will have closure."

After the visit to the garage project, I grabbed a sandwich & then proceeded to my office. I meditated for 30 mins every day. It was a habit inculcated by both my parents at a young age & one that had stuck with me. The meditation centered me & rejuvenated my mind which was very essential in my profession. Normally I meditated in the morning but today morning had been hectic & so I had settled for meditating in the afternoon. I settled on the floor on my yoga mat. As usual I started by concentrating on my breathing & slowly drowning out the other surrounding sounds. Meditation also helped me to direct my thoughts & keep a check on my magic. Today however there seemed to be some kind of a dampening around me which was not allowing me to connect with the universe the way I usually did.

Suddenly, I felt an angry red mist surrounding me. The red haze was acting like a muffler for all my senses & I suddenly felt like my entire body was on fire. Like the mist was trying to suck out the air from my lungs – which felt different than normal suffocation. Years of practice allowed me to calm my mind & control my panic. I mentally pushed back with all my might the way Nani had taught me in my very first lesson. Then I envisioned the cocoon. I imbued my cocoon with a singular intent – protection. Slowly the magic threads started snaking around me. As I focused with my entire being, the threads started connecting & meshing together faster till the only thing left was to seal the cocoon. With a final push of energy, I managed to get the cocoon to seal. But this had taken a lot out of me. As I felt the mist pushed back & got my breathing back to normal, I fell into a deep slumber. The single thought permeating my senses as I drifted off was that this attack felt similar to what I had seen at the restaurant. The realization hitting me that whoever had harmed Mr. Khanna knew that I was somehow a threat & was now intent on getting me out of the way.

In the midst of a restless slumber, I found myself immersed in a dream, a dream that felt all too real. I was in a place where there was no sunlight. It felt like the sepia copy of a very old photo. Shadows danced ominously around me, and an eerie chill hung in the air. I felt a presence, a dark and unsettling presence that sent shivers down my spine. I was pretty sure that I had been summoned to this 'place' wherever it was to send a message. As I peered into the darkness, a figure materialized. I thought it was a woman but it could just as easily have been a man.

"Veena," a voice echoed, a chilling whisper that seemed to pierce through the very core of my being.

"You cannot escape me, for your power belongs to me."

I tried to step back, my heart racing, but it was as if an invisible force held me in place. I mustered the courage to respond, my voice shaking slightly.

"Who are you? What do you want from me?"

The dark entity's laughter resonated, a haunting sound that seemed to reverberate within my mind.

"Names are of no consequence. I am the embodiment of your destiny, the true inheritor of your power. You cannot deny me, for your magic is mine by right."

Fear and defiance swirled within me, mingling like a turbulent storm.

"You're wrong! My power is mine & mine alone. It is my legacy and I'll never willingly give it to you."

The entity's eyes glowed with an otherworldly intensity, fixated on me with an unsettling hunger.

"You may resist now, Veena, but the inevitable is already set in motion. Your strength will be mine, and your defiance will crumble."

Gritting my teeth, I summoned the remnants of my courage.

"I won't be your pawn. My magic is a part of who I am, and I'll fight to protect it."

The entity's laughter grew louder, echoing in the darkness around us.

"We shall see, Veena. We shall see."

With those ominous words hanging in the air, the dream began to unravel, and I woke up in a cold sweat, the memory of the encounter etched vividly in my mind. When I opened my eyes the fading light of the evening filtered through the curtains in my office. I couldn't shake the feeling that the shadowy entity's threat was a harbinger of challenges yet to come.

I mentally thanked Nani for the cocoon & made a cup of coffee with extra sugar for myself. I was still feeling a bit woozy but otherwise ok. I realized that though I had been able to save myself from the red haze, a human might not be as powerful. I needed help to understand this kind of magic & I knew where I would be able to find the answers I sought. While my Nani was knowledgeable in the matters of magic, the force that had guided her & my mother was a magical tome. The ***Tantrika Yogini*** was older than time itself. It contained the history of our race & the roots of our magic. After Ma's death the room which housed Ma's library had been locked by Baba as he believed magic to be responsible for whatever happened to her. The library was housed in the second room in the basement. To get my answers, I would have to unlock the library & get the book. I also needed someone to teach me how to wield my magic. I needed to be able to do more with it than just changing my appearance & cocooning myself. If I was now a target - I needed to be able to launch an attack!

I reached home in time for dinner. Baba & Nani were both in the dining room. Baba doing a crossword while Nani was watching an Insta reel. As I walked in Baba took in my appearance, concern lining his eyes he asked

"What happened Veena beta? Why are you looking so pale? Are you sick?"

With a hint of apprehension, I recounted the harrowing encounter with the red mist to Nani and Baba. Though I knew Baba's aversion to magic, the threat was too close for me to not share this.

Their eyes widened in alarm as I described how the red mist, like a suffocating shroud, had enveloped me, attempting to snuff out every breath. I shivered at the memory, grateful that Nani's teachings had given me the power to create a protective cocoon that shielded me from the malevolent mist's grasp.

"The cocoon you showed me how to manifest—it saved my life." I said looking at my grandmother.

Nani's eyes glistened with an undefined emotion as she listened intently, her hands trembling slightly perhaps remembering something else. Beside her, my father's face was etched with a combination of shock and concern. He seemed to be grappling with the realization of the danger his reluctance to embrace magic had placed us in. But it was the mention of the dream—the entity's ominous words—that struck my father like a bolt of lightning. His expression transformed from shock to devastation, his eyes welling up with tears.

"Veena," he choked out, his voice thick with regret. "I've been so blind. I've let my fear cloud my judgment. I could have lost you today... you too!"

The weight of my father's confession hung heavily in the air, a painful admission of the mistakes he had made.

"It's ok, Baba," I said softly. "Magic isn't our enemy. By shielding us from it, you inadvertently left us vulnerable. We need to learn, to understand, and to protect ourselves."

My father's shoulders slumped, and he drew me into an embrace that felt like a release of years of pent-up emotions. Nani joined in at that moment, the door creaked open, and Varsha stood in the doorway, her eyes wide with a mixture of confusion and concern. Sensing the emotions in the room, she rushed forward, and we enveloped her in our arms, completing the circle of our family.

Chapter 16 – Maya

When I told Nani that I wanted to open Ma's library she was delighted. However, when I mentioned the *Tantrika Yogini*, Nani's face fell.

"The tome is sealed beta. It locked itself the day your Ma died" said Nani with a sigh. "I have tried opening it many times but it does not respond to me. It had a connection with your mother. The same way that a person does" she said as if explaining the book to me.

Apparently, the book had emotions & it also seemed to have a mind of its own. In those early days after Ma's death, it refused to open & then my father had locked the room & the book was lost to us. Now we would have to try to open it again. Nani thought for a bit & then said

"There is only one way that I didn't try then - combining my magic with the magic of its previous mistress's offspring"

"You mean me & Varsha" I asked hoping we would be able to achieve together what she hadn't succeeded in on her own. Nani nodded.

As baba unlocked the door to Ma's library, it was like stepping back in time, into a realm of memories, a sacred space that held my mother's essence. Every shelf, every book seemed to echo with her presence, and I could almost hear her soft laughter and feel her presence beside me. The air in the room crackled with magic, as if the knowledge contained within the books was waiting to be unlocked. Baba felt it as well for he immediately retreated to the floors upstairs as if the force of the memories would cause him to crumple. Nani though resolutely led the way, her steps purposeful and steady. I watched as she traced her fingers along the spines of the tomes, her touch gentle and reverent. But it was the sight of the *Tantrika Yogini* that held a special place in my heart—that drew my attention like a magnet. I could almost see my mother sitting there- at her desk, pouring over its pages, her eyes filled with both curiosity and determination. I approached the tome, my fingers grazing the aged parchment that held centuries of wisdom. The golden filigree on the cover seemed to gleam under the soft light, as if it held a secret energy all its own. Though locked for so many years, there was not a trace of dust on the book. My heart swelled with a mixture of reverence and anticipation. Today, we would open this tome once again, invoking the circle of three—Nani, Varsha, and me.

Nani's confidence was palpable as she explained our plan. The incantations within the tome were sealed with ancient magic, requiring a combined effort to unlock their power. With a shared chant, our voices harmonizing, we would infuse the incantations with enough energy to break the seal that guarded the knowledge within. Varsha stood beside me, her eyes reflecting a mix of excitement and determination. We held hands, forming a circle that connected us not just physically, but also on a deeper, almost spiritual level. As Nani began the incantation, her voice rich, Varsha and I joined in, our voices blending seamlessly with hers. The words flowed from our lips, carrying a sense of purpose and unity. The air seemed to crackle with a subtle energy, and the room itself seemed to respond to our incantation. I closed my eyes, focusing on the rhythm of the chant, feeling the power that surged through our circle, a trinity of generations bound by blood and shared purpose. With each repetition of the incantation, the magical tome before us began to emit a soft, golden glow. The air around us hummed with an otherworldly energy, and I could sense the seal weakening, as if the very fabric of reality was responding to our call. As the final words of the incantation left our lips, the room seemed to hold its breath, a pregnant pause that hung in the air... And then, with a faint, almost imperceptible shiver, the magical tome's cover shifted. The seal dissolved like mist in the morning sun, and the tome lay open before us, its pages beckoning with untold knowledge, secrets waiting to be revealed.

A sense of awe washed over me. We had unlocked the legacy of my mother! As I gazed at the opened book, I felt like it was beckoning to me. Soft whispers & reassurances that could be heard only in my consciousness. It was almost as if my mother had known of this moment in time- like she had left precise instructions with her best friend of what was to be done post her passing for that is what the book felt like to me. The moment my hands made contact with the book cover; it flipped open.

"This is very good beta. The book seems to have a kinship with you the same as your mother" said Nani appreciatively "It has accepted you as its mistress"

Hearing these words, I released the breath I didn't realize I was holding. As I tentatively reached out to touch the ancient tome, a shiver ran down my spine, a mix of anticipation and uncertainty coursing through me. Nani had always believed that this book held more than just words on its pages—it held a connection. A connection to my mother. The moment my fingers brushed against the weathered cover, a sensation unlike anything I'd ever experienced washed over me. It was as if the tome acknowledged the blood tie that linked me to its previous keeper—Ma.

A soft hum resonated through my fingertips, a gentle vibration that seemed to echo in harmony with my own heartbeat. It was as if the tome was alive, a sentient being that welcomed me into its world, inviting me to unravel the mysteries it held within. Closing my eyes, I allowed myself to be enveloped by the energy that emanated from the book, revealing glimpses of knowledge that resonated deep within me. Images and sensations flooded my mind, a dance of insights that seemed to unfold like chapters of a story. The tome revealed fragments of information—ancient rituals, forgotten spells, and secrets that had been carefully guarded through the ages. Each revelation was accompanied by a surge of emotion, a sense of familiarity that tugged at my heartstrings.

In that moment, I felt a profound connection with my mother, a bridge that transcended time and space. The book had been a part of her journey, and now, it was reaching out to me. As I withdrew my hand from the tome, the pages fluttered wildly till the book opened at a particular chapter. The title read "Rakta Pishacha". A sense of wonder and gratitude washed over me. The book had recognized me, and had chosen to reveal what it deemed I needed to know. Nani's words echoed in my mind, her belief in the sentience of the tome now confirmed by my own experience.

"So, this is what we are dealing with" Nani exclaimed nonchalantly probably having anticipated the book's response "Which means that when you mentioned that the mist was pulling air from your lungs- it was not air, it was your life force or your soul. Hence the intense burning because it was trying to suck the soul right out from your body" she continued thoughtfully.

"Yuck! How disgusting!" exclaimed Varsha.

"Do you know what Rakta Pishacha's are?" Nani asked both of us.

"Let me check Google," said Varsha

"Yes, because what better than Wikipedia to give you answers" irritated Nani flicked Varsha's ear.

"What you have open in front of you is the well of infinite knowledge of centuries but you would rather read something on the web?" she asked with disgust.

"But Nani doesn't the web too have infinite knowledge" I asked innocently trying to rile her.

"The web has data. I think you are too wise to not know the difference between the two" said Nani sternly.

"All I remember is that Rakta Pishacha's are considered to be immortal." I recalled from one of my earliest magical lessons with Ma.

"But do you know how they manage to get this immortality?" asked Nani. "You may have heard of the 8 Chiranjeevis in our history. All of them got their immortality either as a boon or through their birth as avatars meant to accomplish specific tasks in the world order. But not so with Pishacha's. They are not inherently immortal rather they steal the life force from others to prolong their life. They can be very cunning & for them the life force of a Rakshasi can sustain them for over a century."

Varsha's eyes had grown to the size of saucers when Nani made this statement.

"But how can they go undetected in this day & age Nani? Wont anyone notice them not dying? What about their birth certificates? Their PAN cards, driving licenses?" She asked.

"These creatures are evil beta. They have been around for centuries you think things like birth certificates or driving licenses are going to stop them? They need to feed but not as often as other creatures. And they can also sustain themselves on partial doses" she said.

"What does that mean?" I asked.

"It means that if they partially drain a human then that person can become paralyzed or grow weak or even go into a coma but not die. If it is a Rakta Pishacha like the book seems to indicate & I would stress on the 'if' for it could just as easily be a witch then it is old - even ancient evil. Pishachas are created when the desire for revenge is more than the desire to save your soul. Since the world has always been harsher on females, most of the Pishachas I have heard of are female," said Nani.

"But what happens after they have taken their revenge?" I asked

"When a human becomes a Pishacha, he or she loses their soul & once their revenge is completed too, they need to consume the souls of others to survive" replied Nani

"The important thing to ask Di is how do you kill one" asked Varsha with an evil glint in her eyes

"Pishachas are powerful but even the most powerful Pishacha is nothing compared to a Rakshasi. You shouldn't have had a problem in the first place if only you would have practiced your magic" said Nani pointedly.

Realizing that Nani was going to make this more difficult than needed, I asked "So basically just go with my instinct right"

"See you already know the answer. Now I have to go for my nap," said Nani

"So, you are just going to let Di 'wing it'" asked Varsha surprised

"Yes, little girl. Don't worry your Di will be fine once she figures who is the Pishacha for they can make themselves look just like humans. I would suggest you do a bit more research" she said indicating to the book.

Varsha possibly sensing my need for solitude, wisely stepped out of the library. I sat at Ma's desk & started reading.

The Rakta Pishacha was folklore for most people & being related to blood was said to be a precursor to the vampire legend in the western lore. While Vampires sucked on the humans & got their immortality through blood, the Pishacha's were more complex. They derived their energy from the human soul itself. They slowly sucked the souls dry of the life force taking them out of the cycle of rebirth. Once a Pishacha got hold of a human's soul, that soul just ended. They were said to be very powerful & like the rakshasa's their energies doubled in the night. The Pishachas were created when a human hungered for revenge. Once a human being became a Pishacha, their soul died. There was also a symbol mentioned in the book - it looked like a serpent eating its own tail. It represented the principle that life consumes life in order to survive and this cycle of creation and destruction continues forever which is symbolic of immortality. I was sure I had seen this symbol before but I could not recall where. I snapped a photo of the symbol on my mobile.

Knowing that I was probably up against a Rakta Pishacha, I also wanted to practically explore the effectiveness of my magic on my own. Nani had mentioned that though we had not practiced magic, it lay dormant in our blood - potent to protect. She was quite sure that the mist would not have been able to hurt me even without the cocoon but she wisely did not voice out the thoughts in front of Baba. If I were to become a regular magical practitioner then his approval was important. Nani had told me this later & also jogged my memory of what had happened when Varsha was threatened as a kid.

After Ma's death, Baba had at first allowed Nani to conduct some magical lessons though reluctantly then that day arrived. Two guys had tried to kidnap Varsha from school. Realizing the danger my sister was in, I had reacted instinctively. My display of magic had not only scared the men but also put Varsha at ease for her to tap into her own magical reservoir. I understood that Nani wanted me to remember the specifics of what had gone down that day.

"You were much more open to your magic when you were younger. When you sensed danger, you reacted instinctively. I think the episode with those goons was a wonderful demonstration of what you girls could do but your father freaked out after that & brain washed you girls to keep your magic under wraps. I too had to modify a lot of memories that day. Had your magic been allowed to grow & flow freely like it should, I have no doubt you would have annihilated your opponent today itself without breaking a sweat" Nani said reproachfully.

I still remembered the look on Baba's face when he saw what Varsha & I were doing. That look & the aftermath of everything afterwards had made me scared of my own magic.

"Look at me Veena" said Nani realizing that I was once again questioning my actions on that day

"You did nothing wrong. Those guys were horrible. You did a favor to all the other girls those 2 probably would have hurt had they managed to escape. Remember you magic is linked to your emotions. If you are scared it will coil itself inside of you. You need to be able to unleash it & you will be able to do that only once you are confident of yourself"

This is exactly what I wanted to test now. I closed my eyes. This time exerting the bare minimal energy to tap into my magic. I murmured the incantations in my mind visualizing the cocoon. Once I could see it, I decided to enlarge it. I wanted to test if I would be able to protect a human. Little by little I fed more magic into the threads forming the cocoon with the intent of expanding it. The threads shimmered & slowly started snaking around each other more loosely. Then more threads branched out till the cocoon encompassed the entire desk. Satisfied with this, I allowed it to dissipate.

The first thing I had thought of when Nani mentioned partial sustenance was Mehul's driver who had been found in a coma. In all the excitement following the funeral & our hurry to get home, I had forgotten to ask Vinay about the driver. I called Vinay.

"Hey Veena, I am in a meeting. Can I call you back?" asked Vinay distractedly.

The police had been unable to make any progress on the case & the department was under a lot of stress. The public was demanding answers. Vinay was working longer hours every day.

"Actually, there is one question I had before you sign off- Who is Raghu & why haven't you told me about him?" I barreled forth with my question before Vinay could hang up. There was a silence at the other end. I was wondering whether I had overstepped when I heard Vinay's voice cautious & tired, asking me

"Who told you about Raghu?"

"I heard some women talking at the funeral. Why would you not tell me about him?"

"We i.e the police have kept him under close observation. His being found unconscious in the parking lot immediately after the murder is very suspicious. It is quite possible that he & Mr. Khanna both were poisoned or he was an accessory to the murderer. We have been told to not release any information pertaining to him"

"I am sorry I didn't mean to ask for a justification from you." I said feeling guilty for putting him on the spot.

"It's all right Veena. I know you are invested in the case. Let me finish my report now. I will see you soon."

Vinay & I were meeting after 2 days as the investigation was keeping him busy. This time we met at the same coffee house but Vinay had gotten along a file. Since the time Nemina & I had mentioned the gas theory, Vinay had widened his search. Though I knew this thread of investigation would lead nowhere, I was hoping that getting more information would enable me to find out the identity of the Rakta Pishacha.

"Out of all Mr. Khanna's clients there was one who died recently. His name was Mr. T. Subramanium. Mr. Subramanium, had threatened Mehul that he would be suing him for malpractice claiming Mehul had stolen funds from him" said Vinay showing me some information from the file.

"However, before that could happen, he had a paralytic attack & was admitted to the hospital."

Another paralytic attack. This seemed to be a pattern I thought.

"He died in the ICU." Vinay continued oblivious to my train of thought "He has a young son who works with a pharmaceutical company in their research wing. I am considering him my prime suspect"

Though Vinay was talking my mind was stuck on the paralytic attack bit. This could not be a coincidence. I was sure that Mr. Subramanium had been killed by the same person who killed Mehul & attacked Raghu & it was definitely not the young man with the pharmaceutical company. It seemed the Rakta Pishacha was feeding more often than what the book indicated.

"You know even if the gas had been released in the restaurant, the murderer would have needed some place to hide the equipment housing the gas. I think we should check out the haunted cottage on the premises of Glocal junction" suggested Vinay.

While I knew that there was no gas & hence no equipment, my mind went back to my last conversation with my sister. Varsha had wanted to explore the cottage with me, though we had never gotten around to it. If I went with Vinay, I was sure that Varsha would throw a fit but it would give us more access to the place with the police badge. It was too good an opportunity to pass up so I immediately agreed.

Chapter 17 – The haunted cottage

"Pinky had called again. I don't know what to tell her anymore. We are doing all that we can. We have valid alibis for all of Mr. Khanna's "business associates" said Vinay as we were walking towards the cottage. He seemed visibly frustrated.

"What about Mrs. Khanna herself? Isn't the widow the first suspect in cases like these?" I asked

"She is if she stands to inherit. Incidentally though Pinky has no solid alibi. She claims she had a headache & was sleeping when the murder took place. I also spoke to Mr. Khanna's lawyer. The way Mr. Khanna's will is structured, Pinky is the guardian but only for their son who has been given 50% of the total estate. The rest get this goes to his daughter" informed Vinay.

This was news to me. Also, I was a bit disappointed since I had assumed that some portion of the money might have been left to Nemina giving her a motive for the murder but that didn't seem to be the case.

"Isn't Maisha also a minor?" I asked.

"She is but only for few more months. Her grandfather has been appointed as her guardian," said Vinay.

"How strange. The elder Mr. Khanna must be over 80 yrs. old. Why appoint him as the guardian?" I said thinking aloud.

"May be Mr. Khanna didn't trust his wife. She is the step mother after all. Now enough grilling me about the case. I thought the cottage tour was a date & no work discussion on a date" admonished Vinay.

I had told Vinay that I wanted to take the haunted cottage tour before examining the premises. He had laughed & then reluctantly agreed saying it would probably be romantic.

We reached the hotel in time for the evening tour of the cottage. There were very few people at this time of the year though I was pretty sure that more people would be coming for these once the vacations started. The plan was to finish with the tour & then explore the cottage for any clues. Our guide was a perky college student by the name of Rahul. He seemed to be reading from a brochure when we arrived. There was only one other girl besides Vinay & me in our tour group & she was only here to spend time with Rahul which was immediately apparent once he started talking.

"As you know, people in this area believe that the cottage I am about to take you to is haunted. There have been sounds of music coming out of what used to be the living area, people also claim to experience a significant drop in temperature when near the cottage. Some have even claimed to have seen the 2 ghosts living there though no one claims to ever have been hurt by them. These are nice ghosts" he said with a smile

"However, the cottage is very old & though the management has made basic structural repairs, I would advise you not to wander anywhere on your own" Rahul continued staring pointedly at Vinay & me.

I nodded in agreement while Vinay just shrugged.

"It sure feels spooky!" exclaimed Vinay.

The girl in the tour group took that as a clue to start chatting

"Doesn't it though. I was so excited when Rahul told me he has started working here. My name is Pallavi. Rahul & I are in the same college. He is my boyfriend" she said to both of us blushing. Rahul too was blushing.

"We plan to finish our project after this tour ends. So, I am hoping we are done early" she continued.

"Actually, this is the last tour for today & I have already checked with the manager" Rahul hurriedly added

"It's ok we are not going to complain. In fact, if you want to start work on your project right away, we can probably see the cottage on our own" Vinay volunteered.

"No. absolutely no one is allowed to be here without a guide supervising. I am sorry," said Rahul.

"Ok then let's get going" I said.

Walking through the overgrown path leading to the haunted cottage, a sense of excitement mingled with anxiety gripped me. As we approached the cottage, its weathered façade exuded an eerie charm, the stories of its tragic past seeming to hang in the air. The cottage was nestled within the same plot as the Gadre's bed and breakfast, a sombre reminder of the fire that had taken lives. I listened intently as Rahul recounted the tale of the Gadres—a childless couple known for their bed and breakfast and the music classes Mrs. Gadre taught. They were healers too, with a reputation for helping those in need. However, it was a tragic fire that forever altered the course of their lives. Both Mr. and Mrs. Gadre perished while attempting to save the lives of those who had sought refuge in their B&B. It was said that their souls remained bound to the earthly realm, unable to find peace. The very thought sent a shiver down my spine, but curiosity got the better of me as we stepped inside the cottage.

The inside of the structure was quite dark & the basic illumination came from 2 bare bulbs hanging from the ceiling which were casting weird shadows around us. The main floor revealed what would once have been a cozy kitchen and a living area. The living area had once served as a space for music classes according to Rahul. I imagined Mrs. Gadre sitting at one end with her harmonium, teaching eager students the magic of music. Vinay motioned towards the sealed bedroom upstairs & Rahul indicated that the bedroom was not structurally sound. After giving us the basic tour, all of us split up to explore the premises. Vinay had informed Rahul that he was the lead detective investigating the murder at the restaurant & that we needed to check the cottage for clues. A relieved Rahul walked away hand in hand with Pallavi presumably to complete their project. He knew the management of the hotel would have no issues with him co-operating with the police.

I decided to explore the kitchen while Vinay went to the living area. Almost immediately, I heard Vinay's voice

"Veena, look at these symbols on the wall. They're unlike anything I've ever seen before."

I went out to the living area to see him pointing at curious symbols etched into a nook in the corner of one of the walls in the main living space. They were put there intentionally & were intricate, almost mesmerizing in their design. My heart raced sensing something familiar in the drawings that my brain either could not or would not process. As I touched the elaborate symbols etched into the walls of the cottage, a rush of memories flooded my mind, pulling me back to a time long ago...

I could almost feel the soft touch of my mother's hand in mine, her voice a comforting melody that lingered in the air like a cherished lullaby. A memory unfolded before me like a forgotten story, I was just a child then. My mother and I had visited this very cottage. It was a time after the tragic fire that claimed the Gadres and a few of the guests at the bed and breakfast. I recalled how my mother had dressed me up in my prettiest frock. I had already been able to see ghosts even back then. So, I asked Ma if we were going to talk to the ghosts of Mr & Mrs. Gadre. She had laughed at my innocent question

"The cottage is a special place, my dear," she had said, her voice gentle and reassuring. "And don't worry, the Gadres have moved on to the next realm. We're safe."

I wanted to tell her that I was not afraid of the ghosts but she seemed to be too preoccupied to listen. Instead, I just nodded. But there had been a purpose to our visit—a purpose that Ma had shared with me. She had explained that she needed something from the cottage, something that required the presence of a young child to serve as a clever disguise. After all, who would suspect a mother with her innocent daughter by her side?

When we stepped into the cottage, Ma had entrusted me with a simple task. I was to stand near the entrance & alert her in case anyone wandered nearby. She had promised me my favourite cherry cake upon our return if I behaved myself. As I waited in the doorway, I could see Ma kneeling down in the space beneath the symbols, her voice a soothing melody as she chanted words that seemed to carry a hidden power. Her hands moved gracefully, tracing invisible threads that connected her to the energies of the cottage. Even now, with my eyes open and the passage of time between us, I could hear her voice echoing within me. As the memory began to fade, I found myself standing in the present, this cottage held secrets, mysteries that spanned generations, and I couldn't help but wonder what it was that Ma had sought all those years ago & if she had found it for the outcome of that trip eluded me...

I clicked a few photos of the symbols & Vinay also did the same for his records. When I wandered back into the kitchen, my attention was drawn to the ancient kadappa platform. I noticed something sticking out from under the platform. It was a white lace handkerchief which looked new & expensive. I pulled it out & noticed that it had a customized design - black lace & a skull embroidered in the corner. It sent a jolt of surprise through me, my mind racing to make sense of the discovery. I had seen a similar handkerchief with Nemina. Would she have come here?

I hastily put the handkerchief in my purse & continued to inspect the space now sure that something had transpired here. I should have shown the handkerchief to Vinay but I wanted to check if the symbol had any meaning first & handing it to Vinay would mean I wouldn't get to see it again. Then I wandered out into what would once have been a garden. There was a mango tree & a kadipatta plant still reminiscent of the kitchen garden which would have flourished here. I was about to call out to Vinay to leave when he snuck behind me & whispered

"There are no ghosts here Veena"

I gave a small yelp

"Vinay! you startled me" I exclaimed.

"Well, if you are going to hang out with a detective, we need to ensure that your senses are sharpened don't we" Vinay exclaimed with a wink.

As we were walking towards the parking where Vinay had parked his bike, his phone buzzed, breaking the otherwise calm ambiance around us. He glanced at the screen with a hint of reluctance before answering the call. I couldn't help but notice the change in his demeanour as he engaged in the conversation. His responses were curt, his tone distant, and a shadow seemed to cast over his handsome face. I sensed that something was amiss the moment he ended the call. My curiosity got the better of me, and I gently probed,

"Vinay, is everything alright?"

He sighed, his expression a mix of frustration and resignation.

"It's my father. He had called to discuss the Khanna case."

I furrowed my brows, concerned by the tension I could practically feel in the air. Vinay never spoke much about his family but I had assumed things were well between them.

"The pressure from your father seems to be getting to you. Is he upset about something specific?" I asked.

Vinay's gaze turned inward; his voice tinged with a bitterness I hadn't heard before. "It's not just about this case, Veena. My relationship with my father has always been... complicated. He's been distant, more of an authority figure than a parent. Even when I chose to become a police officer, it was a battle. He finally relented after realizing I wouldn't back down, but our relationship has never been the same."

I listened attentively, my heart going out to him as he opened up about his struggles.

Vinay continued, "The Khanna case is different. Mr. Khanna's status and the circumstances of his death have turned this investigation into a minefield. My father wants answers from the police, and he's demanding them from me."

Vinay's vulnerability was raw, and my heart ached for the pain he carried. He shared how his decision to join the police had strained his relationship with his father, creating a rift that was only mended partially when his family realized the benefits of having a son in law enforcement. This was why Vinay had moved out to a rented apartment leaving the opulent house his family lived in.

He looked at me with a mixture of longing and determination, revealing a dream he held close. "Veena, that cottage we visited, it made me realize what a real home could feel like—one filled with love and respect. Though now dark & consumed by the ravages of time, the walls still hold the warmth and love that the Gadre's had for each other. Someday, I want to have a place like that- not opulent but beautiful. I want to build a home with someone I love and who respects me in return."

I reached out to gently squeeze his hand.

"Vinay, you deserve a home where you're cherished and understood. And I'm here to support you, no matter where our journey takes us."

He offered me a small smile in return squeezing my hand gently.

After the tour Vinay dropped me back home. I was showing the photos of the symbols to my Nani when Varsha overheard our conversation.

“I knew it! How could you go there without me Di? It was my idea! MY IDEA!” she yelled while stomping her feet.

“Calm down dear girl else Mrs. Joshi will come calling” said Nani with a warning in her tone.

"I am sure your Di had her reasons. Besides we will be going there again so you will get your wish"

Intrigue lined Varsha's face & her anger momentarily forgotten she asked "You mean all 3 of us will be going? And what are those photos?"

She almost snatched the mobile from Nani's hands. Nani had to zing her with magic to retain hold of my mobile

"Wait till I know how to do that! I am going to get even with you" exclaimed Varsha rubbing her sore wrist as Nani smiled.

"I also found this handkerchief there" I said holding out the piece of cloth.

"It is the same design as the one the witch- Nemina carried" I informed Nani.

She held the handkerchief in her hands & observed the skull on it.

"I can't sense any magic on the cloth & I haven't seen this symbol before. However, keep it with you. We can check on it later. The first order of business is to go to the cottage"

"But why is it so urgent?" Varsha demanded.

"Because the Gadre's were Rakshasas. Ma knew them. She had taken me to the cottage when I was around 4 or 5" I announced to a shocked Varsha.

"You are right. The Gadre's were powerful Rakshasas. Their deaths were tragic but heroic. The cottage is a power nexus & the perfect place to teach you the offensive spell you need to learn" Nani refused to elaborate further.

We planned to go on the excursion to the cottage at the earliest.

Chapter 18 – Raghu

Raghu's paralytic attack, Nemina's confession, my visit to the cottage & discovering that it was a power nexus, the information regarding the Rakta Pishacha – these were all related. I could feel that I was very near to solving this. I would have to unravel these threads to solve the mystery of the murder of Mr. Khanna. However, there was one thread that I had not explored at all & it was time to follow it, to check where it would lead. That thread was Raghu.

It had now been almost a week after the murder & the fact that the driver, Raghu had not yet come out of the coma did not bode well for him. Since Vinay had not disclosed any information on his whereabouts, I decided to call Mrs. Pinky Khanna to dig for information on Raghu. I dialed the number she had left me.

"Hello Pinky, this is Veena. Veena Pardeshi. The owner of Parampara designs. You had come down to my office the other day" I began "I was wondering if we could meet. I had seen your house during the funeral & have come up with some design ideas"

I barreled forwards without giving her a chance to respond

"I know you had said that you will be redesigning only after 2-3 months but actually I found something at an auction that I think will be perfect for your house"

After a bit of reluctance, I managed to get Pinky to invite me to her home. I planned to carry a huge Chinese vase I had picked up from an auction in Mumbai. I left my office with the vase in tow & immediately set out for the Khanna residence before Pinky could change her mind. I was ushered into the sitting room by a maid. As I was relaxing on the soft upholstered sofa, I heard Maisha's voice

"What are you doing here?" she asked making no effort to hide her disdain.

"Actually, I had come to meet Pinky- your mother to show her some designs." I said indicating to my folder

"Maisha, that is no way to talk to guests" said Pinky who had probably overheard our conversation as she entered the living room.

"So, you couldn't wait even 5 mins after Papa's death to lay claim to the house & impose your garish taste on us, could you?" Maisha almost spat out the words completely disregarding Pinky.

"Garish like the bracelet you insist on wearing or these skull printed handkerchiefs you carry everywhere?" said Pinky pulling one from Maisha's hands.

I had a jolt of recognition as I recognized the design. The handkerchief was distinctive - white with a skull embroidered in the corner. So apparently Maisha also carried the same skull handkerchiefs as Nemina! That certainly complicated things.

"Give me that. Its mine. Remember -I won't allow you to change a thing till the will is read. You hear me!" yelled Maisha snatching back her handkerchief

"And you" she said pointing to me "do not get entangled in our business if you know what is good for you" saying this she stormed out of the house.

"I apologize for her behavior. She is a teenager what else can I say..." said Pinky embarrassed.

"It's ok. I can understand. She is having a hard time coping with her father's death. If you want, I can come back later"

I reluctantly offered though I would have preferred to have got some information before I left

"When you are doing better" I continued as the maid brought in 2 steaming cups of coffee.

"There is no need for that. After all you have taken the trouble to come down all the way so might as well you show me what it is that you have found? – is this it?" asked Pinky gently picking up the vase I had placed on a side table.

"It is very pretty indeed" she exclaimed seeing the delicate filigree work on it.

I let my gaze wander around the living room & I noticed another black & white photo on the wall which showed the same woman from the photo in Maisha's room posing on her own. In the photo she was sitting on a sofa chair but what intrigued me the symbol hand drawn on the wall behind her. It was similar to the symbol that was in the book on Pishachas but here the serpent was wrapped around a flame.

"That is Mehul's grandmother – Mrs. Padma Khanna. She passed away before we were married but her photo has always hung in our living room. I think Mehul must have been very close to his grandmother" said Pinky when she noticed me staring at the photo.

"Maisha looks a lot like her great grandmother" I remarked. The similarity was so jarring that Maisha could have been the same woman except for the clothing.

"Yes. I have also noticed the resemblance," said Pinky.

"I love the vase but I still need some time before we can discuss the designs" she continued noticing my folder.

I understood that she wanted to dismiss me but was being polite. I was still wondering how to broach the topic of Raghu when the landline rang. The maid answered the phone & called Pinky informing her it was from Well-heal hospital.

"You will have to excuse me. I think this is for our driver Raghu. Such a sweet old man. I hope he wakes up soon though I can't spare any more money for his hospital bills till the will is read" said Pinky as she went to answer the call & just like that, I had the answer of where Raghu was admitted.

As soon as Pinky hung up the call, I made an excuse of another client meeting & took her leave. From the Khanna's house I went straight to the hospital. Enroute, I got a video call from Prakash

"Have all the accessories I had purchased been delivered?" I asked.

"Yes. All of them have been delivered. I have asked my guys to unpack everything taking utmost care. We have also rechecked all light fixtures. The space is being vacuum cleaned - all the surfaces & the upholstery; as we speak & the greens will be delivered in an hour"

Greens was our slang for the plants which I incorporated in all of my designs. They made the place seem alive & I always picked ones which needed the least amount of maintenance.

"The van has already left from the nursery. Now all that remains is your magic touch Veena & then we can do the handover today evening" said Prakash grinning.

In the background I could see his crew finishing up the cleaning. I could spare just an hour at the hospital post which I would have to return to the site.

"Thanks Prakash! I don't know what I would do without you" I said. "I will be there in an hour's time. Man the fort till then" after hanging up with Prakash, I picked up some fresh flowers & headed to the hospital.

Well-heal Hospital was an old hospital in Pune & was reputed for its trust and expertise. Unlike the newer hospital chains, the police could count on the discretion of the hospital staff. That was probably the reason why Raghu had been admitted to this particular hospital. As I entered its standalone building, I was aware of the sense of urgency that is prevalent in any hospital. The ground floor was buzzing with people both staff & patients moving around getting their work done. The reception, billing counters, and the bustling Outpatient Department (OPD) were all on one side of the entrance while a wide staircase leading to the floors above was on the other side along with an elevator & a pharmacy. A placard placed near the elevator gave the general layout of the building.

Most of the people who had come to visit were headed to the general ward located on the first floor. The second floor housed the operation theatres. But it was the third floor that beckoned me—a floor cloaked in a different gravity, housing the Intensive Care Unit

(ICU). Here the atmosphere shifted, charged with the energy of urgent care. This was where I needed to go, to see Raghu &, if possible, to speak with him.

The visiting hours (which were again mentioned on the placard) had drawn to a close so with a quick glance around, I seized my chance. Sneaking past the busy staff, I ascended the stairwell taking care to muffle my footsteps. The corridors on the third floor were hushed. In the silence, my footsteps echoed softly against the polished floors, guiding me toward the ICU.

The weight of what I was about to do pressed against my chest, mingling with anticipation and a tinge of fear of things that could go wrong. I knew that I would have to use magic if I wanted access to Raghu's room. As I neared the double doors of the ICU, I could sense the hopelessness of the families of the patients- some of whom had been in here multiple times. I had to mentally shield my senses to keep the sense of gloom from affecting me. This was a drawback of my ability to read surface thoughts. The negative thoughts, anger & grief if not kept at a distance could literally cripple me.

With a determined breath, I pushed forward, the doors opened into a large passageway. Immediately I was accosted by a ward boy asking me the purpose of my visit. I was informed in no uncertain terms that I would not be allowed to enter. Before he could push me out however, I managed to see that there were 5 rooms on each side of the passage & there was a police guard positioned at the entrance of the 3rd room on the left. I apologized & snuck into the exit for fire escape. Here I used the invisibility spell that I had read in the Tantrika Yogini & slowly ventured in. I noticed that no one was paying me any attention & concluded that the spell must be working. I now had a very tiny time window in which to sneak into Raghu's room. I managed to glide in past the guard & into the room.

There were various probes connected to a pale old man who was lying in the bed. A name tag announced his name as Raghu Jaitley. His eyes were shut & seemed to be sunken in. His breathing though normal was shallow & there was a strange pallor to his skin. I was now convinced that this was the work of a Rakta Pishacha. I was not able to glean any surface thoughts from Raghu other than abject fear. I knew I would have to dig deeper to get the information I needed. I placed my palm on his forehead & used my magic to gently probe through his consciousness. As I mentally projected reassurances of safety & security into Raghu's mind, his fear slowly subsided. I was able to read his thoughts from just before his attack.

"Raghu, I thought you don't smoke?"

I heard a female voice in his mind. The voice came from somewhere behind him as I could not see a face. Raghu had immediately snuffed out the cigarette

"Sorry Madam. It won't happen again"

I could hear him respond. He was turning around when the red mist surrounded him

"Too late for apologies Raghu. I need to feed. If not Mehul, you will have to do for tonight".

I could picture a dark shadow of a woman nearby which Raghu must have seen as his mind faded out of consciousness & fear gripped him. The next thing I heard was the shuffling of feet

"Sir, we have a man down here"

And then a blinding light as more people rushed in.

"Not again... not again"

A frustrated whisper & then total silence. Raghu had been lucky. The police had spotted him before his life force could be completely sucked out. I now knew that whoever the Rakta Pishacha, Raghu had known her personally.

Having gathered all the information I possibly could, I now needed to leave before anyone spotted me. Just as I came out of the ICU & heaved a sigh of relief, I saw Vinay exiting the elevator. There was nowhere to go as our eyes met.

Vinay's piercing gaze met mine and the weight of his anger hit me like a physical force. Before I could even react, he grabbed my hand and pulled me forcefully into the nearby fire escape, away from prying eyes.

"What were you thinking, Veena? How did you even get here?" His voice was low and seething with a mixture of hurt and frustration.

"I had told you explicitly that Raghu is under police protection. You had no right to barge in there like that."

I struggled to match his intensity, my heart pounding against my chest.

"Vinay, I know it may seem impulsive, but I had my reasons. I needed to talk to Raghu, to gain insights that could help us."

He shook his head, his grip on my hand unyielding.

"Your actions could have compromised the entire case. Do you understand the implications of what you've done? Do you know I can arrest you right now for interfering with an ongoing police investigation?"

As my eyes locked onto his, I felt a pang of guilt. But not guilty enough to clue him in on the magical nature of the murderer. A temporary jail cell would have been better than a permanent cell in a mental health institute.

"Vinay, I didn't mean to put the case in jeopardy. I had a different motive."

His frustration seemed to soften slightly, though his grip on my hand remained firm.

"And what motive could possibly justify disobeying a direct order from the lead detective on the case?"

Taking a deep breath, I mustered the most sincere tone I could.

"Vinay, I had gone to meet Pinky today & while there she got a call from the hospital. That is how I knew to come here. Mrs. Khanna mentioned that they couldn't spare any more money for Raghu's medical bills so I wanted to see if I could help. I wanted to offer financial help, to make things easier for his family."

His grip slackened slightly, his anger mingling with confusion.

"You came here to help Raghu's family?"

I nodded, my voice gentle.

"Yes. But when I got to the ICU, I wasn't allowed inside, and I couldn't find his family either. I didn't mean to cause any trouble; I just wanted to make a difference. You aren't really going to arrest me, are you?" I asked in a small voice.

Vinay's expression shifted, a mixture of emotions flickering across his features.

"Veena, I appreciate your intentions, but you can't just act without considering the consequences. Raghu might still be a target, and your actions put him at risk."

I let out a sigh, feeling the weight of his words.

"I understand, Vinay. I truly didn't mean for things to turn out like this."

He finally released my hand, his gaze softening with a hint of regret.

"I'm sorry if I came on too strong, Veena. I just can't stand the thought of you getting hurt."

His words warmed my heart, and I reached out to touch his arm gently.

"I know you're looking out for me, Vinay. I'll be more cautious from now on."

He nodded, "Just promise me you'll stay away from Raghu for now. We don't know what danger he might be in. You have to trust the police on this one. We are doing everything possible to ensure Raghu's safety. I think it will be better if you left from here right now. I will see you in the evening" he said moving towards the ICU.

Though a little hurt by Vinay's behavior, I could understand his anger & decided not to push the issue. When I turned to leave, a young man approached me in front of the elevator.

"Forgive me sister but I overheard the conversation between you & the detective. I am Pratham Jaitley, Raghu's son. My mother is at home & we are taking turns so that one of us is always here when my father wakes up. I wanted to thank you for taking the efforts to come & meet my father. I also wanted to reassure you that currently my company is bearing the medical expenses for my father. You see Mr. Khanna was generous enough to sponsor my education & now I am employed with a reputed MNC. We have good medical coverage" offered Pratham with a strained smile.

As I looked at Pratham, I could see that his father's condition was taking a toll on his health as well. I shook the hand he had proffered & poured whatever soothing magic I could into him.

Suddenly there was a commotion around us. When the ICU doors opened with a nurse hurrying out, I caught hold of her & asked her what was the issue. Though she was reluctant at first, looking at Pratham's anxious face she replied with a smile

"Your father has just come out of the coma Mr. Jaitley" & walked away. Pratham burst into tears of relief as I awkwardly patted his back. Once he had calmed down, he said

"Sister, your presence here has proved to be a very good omen for my father. I am sure now that he will be all right" he smiled at me & went inside as I left from the hospital.

"I really am sorry about what happened at the hospital" said Vinay as he took his seat at the café, we had decided to meet in.

"I just ...couldn't process what you were doing in the hospital. May be next time you can clue me in before you decide to break police protocols" he said with mischief in his voice.

I could see that he was being sincere. Besides I had no right to expect him to understand my reasons for being there when I was keeping so many things from him.

"I will consider it" I responded in a teasing tone "But that is provided you tell me what happened with Raghu & keep me updated on all developments of the case. You have to see that I am already involved in this case Vinay. I need to find the murderer" I said with determination.

"I promise I will keep you updated Veena. No more sleuthing on your own though. Call me if you think you need to investigate something" he said with a serious look. "Incidentally your visit was a lucky omen for Raghu. He has come out of the coma" announced Vinay.

This belief with good omens & bad was a practice prevalent in all cultures but I was not so sure I actually believed in them. What I did believe was that my magic had something to do with Raghu regaining consciousness but obviously I kept that bit to myself as I wondered if it was the manifestation of magic itself which made humans believe in omens. Since humans could not understand the working of the magical realm could it be possible that something deep within their conscience made them react to & notice certain manifestations & mark them as good or evil? As I was pondering on this, Vinay's words interrupted by thoughts.

"He is awake but he wasn't able tell us much. The doctors believe his memory will take some time to return" said Vinay.

This was certainly good news. I elaborated on my meeting with Pratham & told him that I knew of Raghu regaining consciousness. I also promised him that I would keep the information to myself.

"In the meanwhile, we have to explore the angle of the poison gas you mentioned" continued Vinay as I guiltily looked away. "It might be some new weapon that we know nothing of yet. But I think we both need a holiday – I know you have been working hard on your project & this case has been keeping me busy as well so I have planned a mini trip for us tomorrow. I know you will be handing over the keys to Charmie tomorrow so can you take the rest of the day off?" Vinay asked me.

"Sure" I said presuming this was a way for Vinay to make up for his behavior at the hospital.

"What do you have in mind?"

"I would prefer to keep it a surprise," said Vinay

"There is however one bit of interesting information that I can share with you" said Vinay taking a long pause.

I started jabbing his hand with my fork asking

"Are you going to make me beg to tell me the information?" Vinay burst out laughing

"Ok... Ok. I will tell you. Now put down the fork. It hurts you know. Apparently, there is a fixed amount of money that is being transferred to an unknown account from Mr. Khanna's business account for the past 5 years at least & the total amount transferred is quite large. When I informed Mrs. Khanna - Pinky about this, she was totally lost. Poor girl! She has no idea where the money goes."

"Poor girl indeed! Maybe you should take her instead of me on a date tomorrow" I said irritated with Vinay

"Do I detect a sense of jealousy? You know you don't need to be jealous right Veena? This is just the case" said Vinay realizing a bit late as to how his admission sounded.

"The Khannas might need to sell the house if the finances are not sorted" he said concern lining his eyes.

I understood that he was concerned about the family. I had apparently misread his intentions so I decided to let go. Vinay dropped me back taking care to avoid being seen by Mrs. Joshi & promised to pick me up directly from the Poonawala house tomorrow.

Chapter 19 – Spells

That night Nani insisted on going to the cottage of Gadre's saying that I needed to learn to defend myself. At 30 minutes to midnight, she appeared in the living room. Varsha & I were binge watching Netflix to stay up.

"Let's go" she said as she entered " Girls please get my bags" She announced by clapping her hands & pointing to 2 huge tote bags which had magically floated in behind her.

"Do we look like hotel bellhops to you?" asked Varsha annoyed at the clapping

"And what is in these bags? Have you packed for the apocalypse?" she continued "Also why do we need to carry them? Why can't you magically transport the bags to the car?" Varsha continued complaining as she carried out one bag while I carried the other

"We cannot have 2 magically floating bags outside when Mrs. Joshi is keeping watch & we will need everything in those bags. Now don't be a baby & hurry up. We need to reach the cottage by midnight" said Nani as she started walking towards the car.

"Easy for her to say she has 2 coolies with her" grumbled Varsha lugging the tote bag.

My father having had a very busy day had begged off from this adventure & Nani had declared herself to be the designated driver – it was going to be a bumpy ride for sure.

The drive to the cottage was uneventful though we would probably have crossed a few speed-limits & the tickets would be Nani's gift for my father for refusing to come with us. They shared a complex relationship. Nani had cast a spell to make us invisible but it was not needed as the garden & the path to the cottage was empty. I guess the rumors of haunting kept the public away at night which was working to our advantage. As Varsha & I lugged the heavy totes, Varsha grumbling continuously, I noticed that the hotel guards too seemed to avoid this part of the property preferring to take a long route through the boundary.

We dropped the 2 huge totes in the middle of the floor & I switched on the flashlight on my mobile not daring to turn on the bulb. In the pitch darkness of the night, I could sense the power nexus that resided within the boundaries of these walls, waiting to be harnessed. Nani carefully opened her tote bags. The ingredients spilled onto the floor, a diverse array of items that held symbolic significance in the world of magic. Nani's skilled hands moved with purpose; she drew a tantrik yantra in the shape on a triangle on the floor. Then she started placing the various items from the tote bags, each ingredient adding its unique essence to the ritual. Once she was satisfied with the arrangement, Nani began the first part of this lesson - The invoking of white magic.

Nani's hands moved with grace, demonstrating the intricate gestures that accompanied the incantation. As she raised her arms, her fingers splayed in a delicate dance, she asked us to mirror her movements. The movements came naturally as I recalled making them in silly dances with my mother. I wondered for the umpteenth time how my life would have shaped had she been alive. All my senses were attuned to the nuances of each motion. Varsha, too, followed suit, our movements synchronized. I could now feel the magic pulsating beneath my fingers waiting to be unleashed. With a final, resounding utterance, Nani's voice concluded the incantation, and the air seemed to vibrate with the energy we had conjured. My fingers were glowing as were Varsha's & we looked at each other in awe.

"Now comes the more difficult part" said Nani giving a cursory nod to our glowing hands. She now moved to the centre of the triangle she had drawn. I understood that she was invoking the nexus. As Nani spoke, her words seemed to resonate with the very walls of the cottage. Nani's demeanour shifted subtly as she conjured dark magic, her eyes gleaming with an intensity that sent a chill down my spine. The air became charged with an otherworldly energy, and a soft glow enveloped the room as the power nexus responded to her call. The nexus seemed to acknowledge her command.

As the dark magic surged toward us, Varsha and I acted as one. Drawing upon the white magic we had just invoked, we raised our hands, a surge of determination coursing through our veins. The clash of dark and white magic created a dazzling display of colors. I could feel the strain, the effort required to repel the dark magic. Varsha & I channelled our energy into a single purpose—to protect ourselves and harness the light within us. The room seemed to hold its breath as the clash reached its zenith. And then, with a burst of brilliance, the dark magic dissipated. Varsha and I stood, our chests heaving, our hands still raised in a stance of defiance. Nani's proud smile was mirrored on our faces as we realized the magnitude of what we had accomplished. The lesson had come full circle giving us a glimpse of the untapped potential that had always resided within us.

Nani's words carried a warmth as she commended our efforts.

"You have tapped into the essence of white magic—a force that springs from purity of heart and the desire to bring light to the world. Remember, magic is always a reflection of your own intentions good or bad"

As the glow of the power nexus gradually subsided, I realized that we had proven that the power of light could always triumph over darkness if only there was belief. For the first time I felt a confidence in my own power – a confidence which had eluded me from the day I had seen horror reflected on my father's face when I had called him to the school. I recalled now that even as I was protecting my sister, I had mentally reached out to him. That is how he had arrived at the school gates & witnessed the 2 goons suspended in mid-air.

The ride back to the house was anticlimactic with Varsha & I slumped over in the backseat while Nani drove like a lunatic. The late night combined with the magic expended in the lesson had taken quite a bit out of us. I was hoping the 6 hours of sleep I planned to squeeze in would be enough for me to pull through the next day. If not, Vinay would probably get more than he bargained for.

Chapter 20 – The kiss

The next day morning I woke up early. I headed to the Poonawala residence & at precisely 10 am, handed over the keys of the floor to Charmie. She & Anil both walked hand-in hand inside the space.

Handing over the keys to Charmie and Anil Poonawala had I believed unveiled a new chapter of their life story. Their floor in the old bungalow had undergone a remarkable metamorphosis. The marble floors, once lacklustre, now shone like precious gems, having been polished to perfection. As I stood in the foyer, watching Charmie and Anil admire their opal nameplate, a sense of fulfilment washed over me. The peach loveseat which was thrifted from a local shop & upholstered, exuded warmth and hospitality, inviting guests to linger and share in their joy. Opening the ornate double doors revealed a living space that felt warm & inviting. It was designed to showcase the perfect blend of modern elegance without letting go of the hints of tradition reflected in the fabrics & the carefully chosen rugs. I couldn't help but smile as I saw the sunlight pour in through the newly made French windows, casting a warm glow over the room. The mirrors strategically placed around the space reflected not only light but also the happiness that radiated from Charmie and Anil's faces.

I had kept the unveiling of the main area for the last. Leading the couple through a passage into the bedrooms first. Stepping into the lavish master bedroom was like entering a world of dreams brought to life. The chandeliers hung gracefully from the ceiling, their colour-changing lights adding a touch of mystery to every mood. It was a space that called for laughter, conversations, and memories to be made. Each detail & each piece had been lovingly selected for this space keeping in mind the personalities of Charmie & Anil. There was an attached dressing room for Charmie & a separate office space for Anil which were both connected to the bedroom giving them their own little oasis within the shared space.

Lastly, we entered the open-plan living area which was the centrepiece, a haven for celebrations and shared moments. And the Kohinoor of this space was my wallpaper. The rich burgundy contrasted beautifully with the pearl tones of the space. The family tree unfurling with each branch and connection painstakingly etched. The tree's gnarled limbs stretched across the expanse of the wall; their intricate patterns reminiscent of wrought iron gates. The tree bore the weight of old oil portraits (I had chosen these instead of conventional photos. Each portrait a likeness but not an exact replica of the photo), a mesmerizing glimpse into the faces of generations past. The portraits were framed in ornate, gilded frames all printed onto the paper itself but with a 3D effect so that they seemed almost like they could be taken down from the wall. The frames glowed against the deep background. Their sepia-toned hues exuded warmth, as if the faces trapped within the canvas were gently whispering tales of days gone by. The characters portrayed wore the fashions of their respective eras, their poses and expressions capturing their personalities and the spirit of their times. The wallpaper was adorned with delicate, golden filigree which wove its way around the frames, resembling tendrils of ivy weaving through a wrought iron fence. The wallpaper would be a tribute to the roots that ground the Poonawala family. Charmie & Anil were mesmerized on seeing this & stood rooted to the spot till I called out their names.

"I take it that you like the wallpaper then" I said with a satisfied smile.

As Charmie and Anil showered praise upon me and my team, my heart swelled with a sense of accomplishment. I could hardly believe the journey from concept to reality, and I knew that this project would forever hold a special place in my heart.

Charmie bubbled with excitement as she informed me that she would be showcasing the new space to her friends on Friday evening

& I was invited to the kitty party. Only after assuring her that I would be there was I allowed to leave for my picnic date. Vinay picked me up finally announcing that we were going to Mahabaleshwar.

The sky was slightly overcast hinting at drizzles later in the day typical of the season as Vinay and I hit the road for a much-needed escape to the hill station. Since Vinay had insisted on labelling our outing as a picnic (as if we were starring in some Bollywood rom-com), I had dressed for the part in a flowy beach dress with a large straw while Vinay rocked a casual button-down shirt. Considering the season, I had also packed a change of clothes.

"So, what's on the agenda for today, my handsome guide?" I quipped, eyeing him with a smirk.

He shot back a playful grin.

"Well Ma'am, we'll be checking out some touristy spots, pretending to be culture enthusiasts, and attempting to survive the overwhelming 'selfie-taking' crowds. I will also expect to be paid for my services"

I chuckled & decided to play along.

"Great. What sort of payment will you take"

"No cash or card only hugs & kisses" said Vinay with a wink as I rolled my eyes at his cheesy one-liners.

We hopped around, posing for pictures like overenthusiastic tourists & embarrassingly our sightseeing escapade included more selfies than I cared to admit. By lunchtime, our growling stomachs led us to Mapro Gardens, where we indulged in a strawberry overload. Vinay teased me mercilessly as I snapped Instagram-worthy shots of strawberry ice cream, strawberry shakes as well as me inside a big strawberry booth.

"Are you starting a strawberry appreciation page or something?" Vinay teased me, raising an eyebrow.

I shrugged, unapologetic.

"You never know, it could be the next big thing."

Just as we were about to dig into our strawberry-themed lunch, a few raindrops began to fall, interrupting our meal. We looked up at the sky in surprise as the rain drops started to pelter us.

"Well, isn't this a refreshing twist to our perfect picnic plan?"

I said with a laugh, my hair starting to get damp from the rain. I had taken off my cap to enjoy the breeze. Vinay grinned, shaking his head.

"Leave it to Mother Nature to keep us on our toes. At least we have a change of clothes."

With our food hastily covered and our laughter ringing in the air, we embraced the unexpected rain shower, turning it into an impromptu dance party. The raindrops glistened on my cheeks as I twirled around, my heart light with the sheer joy of the moment. After our al fresco meal, we decided to hit the lake for some boating action. I challenged Vinay to a race, declaring myself the undisputed Queen of Paddle Power. Each of us would paddle for the maximum duration while letting the other person rest. We would time our paddling time & the one who paddled the longest would win. After about 30 mins, it was my turn to paddle. But I got tired in 20. Not wanting to lose I shamelessly employed magic to paddle for me beating Vinay's record by 5 mins.

"Wow, Your Highness, you've truly outdone yourself this time," he deadpanned as we docked the boat though he seemed a bit annoyed to be beaten.

As the sun began to set, Vinay & I drove to a cliff that boasted an incredible view. I leaned against the railing, my heart racing as the moment hung between us. Vinay nudged me playfully.

"You know, I heard this is where all the heartthrobs bring their dates for the 'romantic sunset view' experience."

I shot him a sarcastic glance.

"Oh, I'm swooning already."

But then, his voice turned soft, his tone genuine.

"Seriously, Veena, I brought you here because I wanted a moment away from the chaos. Just us."

I felt a warmth in my chest, the snarky banter giving way to a connection that felt real. His fingers brushed against mine, and the world seemed to slow down.

"Veena," he began, his voice tinged with something deeper, "there's something I've been meaning to do. And this time there will be no interruptions"

Before I could respond, his lips met mine in a kiss that sent shockwaves through me. I was so taken aback that I almost forgot to kiss him back. Almost.

We pulled away, breathless, our eyes locked. "Well, that was unexpected," I quipped, a mischievous grin playing on my lips.

Vinay smirked, his dimples showing.

"Expect the unexpected, right?"

As the rain shower continued to sprinkle droplets around us, the sky was lit up with orange hues of the setting sun. The weather was wonderful & the view was incredible with the whole valley spread beneath us. Vinay slowly took my hands in his as we stood still taking in the beauty surrounding us. Suddenly I heard a ringing in my ears. We were literally in the middle of nowhere so there was no chance of this being anyone's ringtone. There was no range here. I realized that the ringing was in my brain as if warning me of imminent danger. I saw a fleeting glimpse of a hospital room. Raghu was in danger & we needed to head back.

"I ... I think I am sick" I said.

"What happened?" asked Vinay "Is it the cold? Or the food? What do you want me to do?"

"Take me to the Well-heal hospital. I need a doctor." I said clutching my stomach.

I did not want to lie to Vinay but there was no way he would believe me if I told him that Raghu was in danger & this was the easiest way to get us there in time. Since starting to actively engage my magic, I had found that there was a lot I could do. The warning in my head being one of the things that no longer surprised me. Lying to this extent & looking at Vinay's anxious face was making my stomach plumet for real though. Vinay drove at the speed limit & got us to the hospital in record time.

When we reached the hospital, I told Vinay that I wanted to go to the restroom. In the time that he went to search for the doctor, I managed to sneak up to the 3rd floor where Raghu was still being kept under observation. The scene that greeted me proved that my assumptions were correct. There was 1 doctor & 1 nurse in the hallway who both seemed to be dazed. The families of the patients who had a separate waiting area were all dozing & the guard kept to guard Raghu's room was slumped in his chair. There was a figure standing beside the guard & I could make out that it was a young girl or a young woman but she was wearing a hijab so her face was not visible. I rushed towards the figure but the moment she realized I was there; she ran towards the other end of the passage towards the emergency exit. I gave chase but by the time I reached the guard the girl was long gone & I could see that the police guard was having some sort of seizure. I somehow managed to lay him on the ground & laid a protective shield encompassing the room entrance & the guard. Then I ran down to get help. By the time I came back with the doctor the guard was unconscious. Dr. Majumdar immediately called Vinay to report the incident.

When Vinay rushed upstairs & he saw me there was a big question mark on his face; but he was a detective first so he started with the interrogation asking me to wait till he was done with the others. The stories of the other people were what I expected them to be most of them had just fallen asleep though they could not be certain why. The 2 who were awake did not remember much. I could sense Vinay's frustration as he finally came up to me to take my statement.

"How are you feeling now?" he asked sarcastically but I could feel the hurt beneath it.

"Better. Actually, I was throwing up when..." I started trying to stick to my illness story

"When what Veena? You had a sudden urge to come up here? I think there is something you are hiding from me but for the life of me I cannot figure out what it is..." Vinay was intently looking at me.

I wanted to confide in him so much it hurt, but then I remembered Nani's words. I could not afford to expose my family...could I?

"I just... I was feeling better after throwing up & wanted to see Raghu before we left" I finished lamely.

Vinay seemed to be disappointed with my response.

"Ok. Don't confide in me if you don't want to"

I could hear the hurt in his voice & my eyes were welling up as well. I swiped at them vigorously lest the tears give away my state.

"I think the murderer tried to kill Raghu again today. I saw a woman in a hijab when I exited from the elevator" I said desperate for him to understand.

"Ya. I got a similar description from the doctor. He remembers seeing a woman in a hijab asking him Raghu's room number but he can't recall much after that" said Vinay "It's good that he can corroborate the presence of another woman & the CCTV footage also shows her else I would probably have had to arrest you for attempted murder" he said jotting down my statement & refusing to meet my eyes.

"You don't honestly believe I am a murderer do you Vinay?" I asked trying to get him to look at me

"I don't know what to believe anymore Veena. My heart doesn't believe that you are capable of killing another human being in cold blood. But I can't keep wondering what you're up to, always putting yourself in danger without considering the consequences!" Vinay's words cut through me, and I felt my heart break a little.

"I think its best we don't meet again" said Vinay still avoiding my gaze. "I cannot be with someone who doesn't trust me" he said in a forlorn voice "I have recorded your statement. You are free to go"

"But... what about Raghu? And the guard? Is he going to be ok" I asked desperate to continue the conversation.

"This is a police matter. Best you leave it up to us" saying this Vinay turned away from me & headed in the direction of Raghu's room leaving me standing in the hallway.

As I stood alone in that hospital corridor, I couldn't help but wonder if my determination to protect Raghu had cost me the one person I had come to care for deeply. I rushed to the restrooms & gave way to my tears. While I knew this was bound to happen, I had always believed I would have more time before confiding my secret. Now that time was long gone. After I had cried myself out, I headed home.

Varsha who was home took one look at my face & understood something was wrong. She brewed a cup of coffee for me just the way I liked it & then said

"No one deserves so many tears Di. What did that fool do?"

"He didn't do anything Varshu. It's not his fault that I am unable to confide in him. Any sane human being in his position would have done the same thing"

I narrated the whole episode with Raghu to Varsha.

"Hmm... so what Di? There are some things you need to accept on faith. He shouldn't have asked for an explanation & put you in a position where you felt like you needed to lie"

Varsha was my sister & loved me unconditionally but I didn't think putting the blame for what happened on Vinay was helping anyone.

“He will come around if he knows what’s good for him,” continued Varsha darkly.

I was too tired to argue & begged off the magic lessons for the day before slumping in my bed & drifting off to dreamland.

Chapter 21 – Malevolence

I spent the next 2 days moping around in the house & taking only the most pressing calls regarding the Gupta's project from Prakash. Baba was mostly ignoring me- not able to decide if what had happened was for the best or the worst while both Nani & Varsha were frustrated with me & were threatening bodily harm if I didn't go to office the next day. My magic lessons were not going well which was unsurprising. Neither was my meditation for I could not concentrate. The second night changed all of that.

After a pathetic attempt at replicating the burst of white magic that Varsha & I had unleashed at the Gupta's cottage, I had received a severe tongue lashing from Nani who had threatened to stop my lessons if I couldn't pull myself together.

"I have not raised a loser! Stop pining over one guy" she had sternly reprimanded me.

My dreams that night were disturbed. The shielding that Nani had taught me had seemed to keep the entity which I believed to be the Rakta Pishacha out of my mind. But tonight, my grief had possibly lowered all my defenses & somehow, she had managed to sneak in again. I found myself once again trapped within the enigmatic realm of my dreams, a place where shadows played their cryptic games and whispered secrets I struggled to decipher. And amidst the swirling darkness, she emerged – the sinister entity that had haunted my sleep before. A shiver ran down my spine as I braced myself for the unsettling encounter.

"Why do you persist, mortal?" Her voice slithered through the air like a chilling whisper, sending a shudder through my core. "Your interference wearies me."

Despite the fear coiling in my chest, I steadied my voice. "I won't stand idly by while you prey on innocent souls."

A harsh, mocking laughter filled the air. "Innocence is a fleeting concept. Souls are mere sustenance, and I hunger."

My fists clenched at my sides, determination surging within me. "I won't allow you to extinguish their light."

Her form shifted within the shadows, and a twisted smile seemed to stretch across her dark features. "You've already meddled, haven't you? Protected that insignificant soul named Raghu. And now, another must suffer for your audacity."

My heart raced as her words struck me like a chilling wind. "No! I won't let anyone else pay for my choices."

Drawing closer, her presence felt suffocating, an embodiment of the darkness she represented. "Your defiance is meaningless. Embrace your place, insignificant one. Allow me to feed, and perhaps I shall spare you."

My determination only solidified; my voice unwavering. "Or what? You know what you are? You are a coward! Hunting under the cover of darkness. If you have so much faith in yourself then come forth in the light of the day & I shall fight you."

A growl of frustration emanated from her, a surge of anger rippling through the shadows. "You'll come to rue this defiance, mortal. When we do meet, you shall know the depths of despair."

And with that ominous declaration, the entity dissolved back into the murky darkness, leaving me standing alone in the dream world.

I woke up feeling more tired than when I had gone to sleep, the last words of the entity still echoing in my conscience. I decided to err on the side of caution. I called up Pratham & checked up on Raghu who was slowly regaining his health but still hadn't been able to recall any additional details. I also called up Pinky & made general chit chat guessing that if there was anything untoward happening, she would hint at it. Then it was time to get on with the day. I once again tried to meditate & after about 15 mins gave up.

Today was the day of the kitty party & I needed to put my best foot forward. Now was the time to make the new connections which would propel my business to the next level. Charmie had sent out invites to all her friends & acquaintances for the kitty party at her new pad. I took an extra long hot shower to wipe away the remnants of the dream & then headed to my office to finalize on the designs for the garage conversion. The Guptas had received permission for the second floor & the material needed to be ordered in this week if we were to meet the timeline.

After working in my office through the morning, I came back home in the afternoon to get ready for the party. I opted for a peach silk kurti with minimal thread work which was neither over the top nor I hoped, too casual for the occasion. I was a little nervous about meeting the ladies but confident in my work. I had chosen a single line antique pearl choker as my only jewelry for the evening. I was also carrying plenty of business cards for the occasion. Anil as well as his father had wisely opted decided to stay out late planning a business dinner to coincide with the kitty party.

I arrived 20 mins before the time mentioned in the invite & was informed that both Charmie & her MIL were still getting ready. The serving staff had already started with the starters. The mini finger sandwiches & the cheese palak samosas were Yummy. As were the various mocktails being offered. I settled with some pina-colada & started browsing through the guest list. Towards the end I saw the name Mrs. Pinky Khanna. Curious I was about to start searching for Charmie to check if it was the same Mrs. Khanna when the hosts stepped out.

Charmie chosen ensemble was a striking fusion of traditional Indian and contemporary Western wear, a reflection of her eclectic taste. She looked elegant & chic in her indo-western dress which featured a sleeveless blouse with intricate embroidery that shimmered in the soft glow of the venue. The deep neckline added a touch of modernity, while the delicately embellished sheer fabric in vibrant hues of peacock and silver resonated the rich heritage she embodied. The skirt combined the elegance of a lehenga with the flair of a flowing gown. A slim, intricately beaded belt that cinched her thin waist, added a contemporary touch while completing the ensemble. The Senior Mrs Poonawala had gone the more traditional route. Her handwoven silk saree was a masterpiece of artistry, the rich texture begged to be touched. The deep emerald green hue complemented her regal aura, her blouse had delicate embroidery which traced intricate patterns along the neckline and sleeves. Both women had adorned themselves with exquisite jewellery – possibly heirlooms. Charmie was wearing a statement diamond set with matching jhumkas & Mrs Poonawala sported an emerald set in kundan. Next to this opulence I felt woefully under dressed in my pearl necklace & my silk kurti. I set a mental reminder to self - to invest in designer outfits to fit in at high society parties should I land another such project. Charmie however embraced me warmly the moment she saw me. Then she stood by my side & started introducing me with genuine enthusiasm to the various ladies who had started arriving to celebrate the occasion.

"Veena, allow me to introduce you to our lovely guests," Charmie beamed, gesturing towards a middle-aged lady "This is Mrs. Mehta, the brilliant fashion designer I was telling you about."

Mrs. Mehta's stylish outfit spoke volumes about her line of work. I extended my hand with a warm smile. "It's a pleasure to meet you, Mrs. Mehta. I've heard so much about your remarkable work."

Mrs. Mehta's eyes sparkled as she shook my hand. "Likewise, Veena. I must say, your design work here is absolutely breathtaking. The Poonawala family tree wallpaper is unlike anything I've ever seen."

"Thank you so much," I replied, feeling a rush of pride. "I wanted to create something unique that would truly reflect the Poonawala family's heritage."

As we were conversing, I noticed intricate kundan & bead work on the bodice of the Indo-western sharara suit that Mrs Mehta was wearing. Once again, this outfit was a masterpiece in itself, tailored to perfection, and I couldn't help but marvel at the exquisite craftsmanship. I felt a twinge of envy as I realized that her attire likely cost more than what I had made on the entire Poonawala project. The good thing though was that my work was finally getting noticed in the right circles. Mrs. Mehta's admiration for my work was evident, and we delved into a lively discussion about the fusion of design and fashion before she was called by one of her other friends. As she excused herself, I continued to circulate amongst the guests.

A few steps away, Mrs. Wadia who Charmie had informed me owned a restaurant, caught my attention. Her kantha work saree was a work of art, and I couldn't help but compliment her choice. Every woman here had taken extra effort to look their best for the occasion.

"Your saree is exquisite, Mrs. Wadia," I remarked, genuinely impressed. "The intricate details are simply mesmerizing."

She laughed heartily; the sound infectious. "Ah, thank you, Veena! Sarees are my passion, and I believe they're a canvas for expressing our individuality."

"That's a beautiful way to put it," I replied, admiring her perspective.

Mrs. Wadia leaned in conspiratorially. "You know, we're planning a renovation for my restaurant soon. I'd love to have your insights and ideas."

I felt a surge of excitement. "I'd be honoured to help, Mrs. Wadia. Let's definitely discuss it further."

As the evening unfolded, I found myself immersed in engaging conversations with many accomplished women. The discussions ranged from design inspirations to the nuances of creativity. I had handed out 4 business cards & sent out numerous WhatsApp messages with my details when I noticed Pinky observing the family tree wallpaper. She did not seem to know many people at the party & was standing alone nursing a drink. I excused myself from the lady I was chatting with & walked over to her.

“This is quite lovely” she said indicating the family tree. “It reminds me of the Harry Potter movie but this one is more aesthetic because instead of the photos I think you have used miniature portraits”

"Yes, that is correct," Pinky was only the second woman who had remarked on the Harry Potter link, the other being Charmie herself. I presumed this would be because the other ladies were not familiar with the details in 'Harry Potter' books.

"The portraits went better with the overall design aesthetic. These have been inspired by old newspaper clippings" I responded to Pinky noting her astute observation. I had a sneaking suspicion that this woman was not as dumb as she portrayed.

"I would love to have something similar done but Mehul's family tree can only be traced back 2 generations. Besides there are no birth or death records for some members. For example, there is no death record for his grandmother. Whenever I asked Mehul about his grandmother, he would change the subject. I presume her death would have been traumatic but there was never any Shradha for her. Only for Mehul's mother, his first wife & his grandfather. And while I know the birth date of Maisha is January 15th, I was never able to find any birth certificate for her either when I was checking the documents after Mehul's death. And I know my husband was meticulous for documentation," said Pinky. She really had given this a lot of thought.

The documentation remark triggered something in my memory – the untraceable monthly transfers that Vinay had told me about of which Pinky claimed to have no clue. Just as I was about to ask Pinky about them, she got a call. When Pinky checked the number displayed on the screen, worry lines appeared on her face. As she answered the call, her eyes widened & her forehead furrowed at whatever was being said at the other end of the line. The cheerful ambiance seemed to dim around me as a sense of foreboding overtook all my senses. My heart raced as I hoped fervently that this time, no more tragic news had struck the Khanna family.

From Pinky's tone of voice, I could sense that something was very wrong. I had arrived at the party in a cab, knowing that indulging in cocktails would render me incapable of driving back. Little did I know that the evening would take a sudden turn, casting a shadow over the festivities.

"Veena," Pinky's voice quivered as she turned to me, her eyes filled with distress. "I... I need to go home. Something's wrong with Sanish's nanny, she's missing, and my cook called to tell me."

She clutched my hand & continued

"Can you please come with me? I don't know anyone here & I could use a friend right now"

"Sure. Let me just inform Charmie"

I replied glancing at her worried face. My heart sank, my instincts whispering that this was more than a simple misunderstanding. I excused myself from Charmie and quickly informed her about the unexpected turn of events, apologizing for my abrupt departure

As Pinky and I hurriedly made our way out of the house, alarm bells of all kinds had started overwhelming my senses. Pinky's driver drove us to the Khanna residence. Pinky was already dialing Vinay's number by the time we entered the driveway. Her voice trembled as she spoke

"Vinay, it's Pinky, Sanish's nanny is missing, and... and strange things have been happening since Mehul's murder. I can't file a report yet, but please, can you come over?" I heard her say.

"Vinay is on his way. I feel so safe when he is around. His strong presence is a great comfort for me you know" she said looking at me as I patted her shoulder dreading the thought of coming face to face with Vinay again.

When we entered the house, the staff was in the living room & all of them looked a bit panicked.

"I checked all the rooms Ma'am but Mrs. Khurana is nowhere to be found. We have been trying her mobile but no one is answering" said Malti, the same maid who had served me tea.

"Could she have gone to get vegetables or milk & lost her mobile" asked Vinay as he entered the house just behind us.

"Oh Vinay! Thank you so much for coming" said Pinky hugging him.

Their physical contact was like a knife straight to my heart. Vinay awkwardly returned her hug & looked at me.

"I asked Veena to come with me. I needed a friend & she graciously agreed to come here with me" said Pinky anticipating Vinay's unasked question.

"Let me search the house once" said Vinay "Not that I don't trust anyone here" he added hurriedly "This may just be a false alarm. She may have gone to visit her relatives or something & just forgotten to inform anyone."

"Mrs. Khurana's room is on the 1st floor at the end of the passage" volunteered Sunita.

As Vinay was about to mount the stairs, the gardener rushed in. He looked very scared.

"Madam... Mrs. Khurana... inspector please come with me" he said grabbing Vinay's hand & dragging him outside.

As we followed the gardener, we reached a mango tree in one corner of the garden towards the back of the house. A lady in her late 40s or early 50s was sprawled beneath the tree - Mrs. Khurana. Her eyes were open & staring into nothing leaving no doubt that she was very much dead. She was also foaming at the mouth. Besides me Pinky gave a tiny shriek & fainted.

Chapter 22 – Another victim

Amidst the chaos, a chilling realization pierced my consciousness – the Pishacha had claimed another victim just as she had promised!

Pinky's delicate figure swayed, and before I could react, Vinay's strong arms swooped in to catch her. He lifted her with ease, his actions swift and decisive, as he carried her into the house and gently laid her on the sofa.

"Are you alright, Pinky? Take a deep breath" instructed Vinay "Can someone please get a glass of water?" he asked.

A pang of mixed emotions gripped me as I watched Vinay, sadness for the dead woman, dread for the Pishacha & jealousy for the frail beautiful woman draped over his arms. Even in this situation, I found it difficult to muster concern or even sympathy for Pinky, especially when she was batting her doe eyes at a man who still held a piece of my heart.

All the staff seemed to have frozen with fear on hearing about a death in their midst & no one had fetched the water. Taking advantage of the situation I decided to remove myself from the immediate vicinity of the drama unfolding before me. I asked Malti the way to the kitchen & went inside. Sanish was seated at the kitchen counter eating cookies while the senior Mr Khanna, his grandfather waited nearby. I was thankful that at least someone seemed to have enough presence of mind to keep the child engaged. I smiled at the old man but he did not seem to remember me. As I came out with the glass of water, I could hear the tail end of Vinay's conversation on the phone

"...Yes Aniket, get the medical examiner also with you. The body is in the garden & I have instructed everyone to not contaminate the scene" as he hung up the call, Vinay wordlessly took the glass of water from my hands & offered it to Pinky.

Vinay's request for everyone present to remain put was met with a collective nod of understanding. As I glanced around at everyone who had gathered, I noticed that Maisha was nowhere to be seen. I felt it prudent to point this out to Vinay so that the girl could be brought home. The Rakta Pishacha seemed to be targeting this family & no one was safe anymore. Despite the awkwardness that lingered between us I felt compelled to share my observation with Vinay

"Vinay," I began tentatively, my voice carrying a mix of hesitation and concern. "I couldn't help but notice... Maisha is nowhere to be seen. She's not here."

"Oh my god" exclaimed Pinky "Maisha has gone for a trek. She will be back day after tomorrow & she had informed us that she will be in the hills with no cell phone coverage. How do we tell her what has happened? Mrs. Khurana was close to both the kids"

She started sobbing. Vinay raised his hand to pat her shoulder to offer support but I could no longer suppress my emotions. As Vinay's hand made contact with Pinky's shoulder, both of them yelped in pain & Vinay got pushed back from Pinky as if by an invisible force. Pinky raised her head & for a fleeting moment I felt like she was actually smiling but when I looked carefully, her face had gone back to its morose expression. May be the light was playing tricks. Vinay on the other hand was rubbing his palm murmuring something about static. I knew he was trying to explain away what had happened the only way he knew- with logic & science. Sensing that I needed to get my emotions under control, I excused myself & went to the guest washroom.

After several splashes of cold water on my face I felt refreshed & once again in control of my emotions. By the time I exited, inspector Aniket Jadhav had arrived at the scene. The police had asked all the staff members to gather in the garden while the family was asked to stay in the living room. As the police started recording the witness statements, I felt a sense of déjà vu of the scene in the restaurant.

Murders with swirling mists, evil spirits invading dreams, fainting heroines, heroic detectives, and a missing teenager to top it all – it felt like I had stumbled into a supernatural soap opera! Each twist and turn revealed a new layer of intrigue and absurdity. Oh, how my sister would have loved to be centre stage here - the joys of reality, where life imitates the most entertaining forms of fiction. I sarcastically thought. Vinay had divided the staff & the other members of the house into two factions to make it easier & faster to question them. One would group would be handled by Vinay himself & the other by Aniket. When Vinay told Aniket to take my statement, I felt it was deliberate avoidance on his part.

Aniket seemed to be aware of the tension between us. As soon as Vinay was out of earshot he asked

"I have never seen Vinay as dejected as he has been the past two days. Have you guys had a fight?"

I was quite surprised at the question. I wasn't aware that Vinay had told other people about us.

"Don't worry" said Aniket as if reading my mind "Vinay & I have been working together for the past 3 years. We are very good friends. He hasn't told everyone at the station about the you."

I was relieved on hearing this. I did not want other people especially the police to ask me any additional questions. But I liked Aniket so I decided to answer as honestly as I could.

"I think we are just fundamentally very different people Inspector Jadhav - I don't think it would have worked between us" I said without going into the details as I looked at Vinay's profile.

On closer inspection I could see dark circles under his eyes & at least 2 days of stubble. In a way his appearance made me feel glad to know that I was not the only one suffering.

" Veena, can I call you Veena? And you can call me Aniket" I nodded "I think whatever issues you may have had; they are not as big as the 2 of you seem to think they are. I have seen my fair share of couples & I have also seen Vinay with his previous girlfriends. It was different with you. With you he was the best version of himself." I was touched at the sincerity in Aniket's voice.

"You have shifted his reality, Veena. I think he just needs time to accept the shift – else I have a feeling that he will not be able to solve this case" said Aniket cryptically. He looked at me as if about to ask a question but then seemed to rethink.

"Things will work out. Have faith." He patted my shoulder & then proceeded to take my statement. How strange that having faith was exactly what I had asked from Vinay.

The medical examiner had estimated that Mrs. Khurana had been dead for at least 3 hours before her body was discovered. I found this hard to believe but when Pinky told me that Sanish usually took a nap in the afternoons, things became clearer. Apparently, Mrs. Khurana had put him to sleep as usual around 4 pm but had not gone to wake him up at his usual time. The child had woken up on his own & wandered into the kitchen at 7.30pm. Pinky had left for the party at 6.15 pm but no one had seen Mrs. Khurana after 4.30 pm since she usually caught up on her TV in her own room when Sanish slept. Basis this information, the time of death had been fixed between 5.30 pm to 7.30pm. Since I was busy hobnobbing with multiple social butterflies in that time span, my statement was brief & my alibi airtight. Currently the police had multiple suspects & no witnesses.

As I was giving my statement, I saw Vinay observing me from afar but when our eyes met, he averted his gaze. I sat with Sanish telling him stories & jokes to keep him entertained as the police took statement of everyone. Vinay also contacted Mrs. Khurana's niece who was her only living relative & informed her about her aunts' death. She was told to collect the body from the morgue after the post mortem. I already knew that in this case too they would not be able to find a cause of death.

Pinky had managed to find the details of the company which had organized Maisha's trek but when Vinay called them, the guy on the line mentioned that Maisha had never joined the group which she was assigned to. Maisha's disappearance had heightened the criticality of the situation & at Vinay's insistence, a police guard was placed at the Khanna bungalow for the night. Though Pinky said that Maisha did sometimes take off & stay with friends, calling her best friend also yielded no results. Pinky was so distraught by this time that Vinay had to call her doctor who immediately gave her a sedative. Meanwhile, Mehul's father had called his cousin sister to stay with Sanish.

By the time Mrs. Khurana's body had been taken to the medical examiner's office & the police had taken the statements of all the staff members, it was quite late.

"Let me drop you home" offered Vinay as I walked outside to catch a rickshaw. It was quite late in the night & the lane was deserted.

"Thank you, Vinay, but I think I can manage. I will get a rickshaw from the main road" I said.

"Please just let me drop you home" said Vinay in a pained voice "or at least let me accompany you till the main road".

I was about to refuse again when I had a feeling of being in danger. All my senses were on full alert & the hair on the back of my neck stood on end.

Chapter 23 – Revelations

Vinay's words of concern about the late hour were like a familiar tune, which warmed my heart. His concern was evident from his actions though he would refuse to acknowledge it. The stillness of the night which had wrapped around us was broken only by the distant melodies of chirping crickets. Just as I was about to respond to Vinay, a sudden surge of magical energy rippled through my senses, jolting me into alertness. Without a second thought, I summoned a protective shield around both Vinay and me, enveloping us in its shimmering embrace.

The gunshot-like sound of a bullet striking the magical barrier echoed in the silence, a distinctive pop that felt surreal in the night air. Suddenly, a masked figure burst out of the foliage & started running in the opposite direction. Instinct guided me, and I projected another layer of magic, this one forming a sparkling net that entrapped the attacker within its confines. He struggled within the magical constraints, caught in a bizarre spot-jogging motion, his escape thwarted. Vinay who had been walking besides me did not understand what had happened. He was kneeling on the ground examining what looked to be a bullet. He slowly lifted his eyes & noticed our masked assailant running but not being able to cover any distance. A gun, possibly the same one which had fired the bullet had fallen nearby.

Vinay's eyes widened, a mix of astonishment and bewilderment.

"Veena, what just happened?"

His question was tinged with the weight of accusation and confusion. I could see the hurt in his eyes, his trust seemingly betrayed by my silence about this hidden aspect of myself.

"What the hell Veena! What did you do?"

Vinay asked again for he could not believe what he was seeing with his eyes.

My voice held a mixture of regret and resolve as I sighed softly.

"Vinay, I know it seems like I've kept something from you, and I'm genuinely sorry for that. But right now, we have more pressing matters at hand."

"No! This... this is not normal. Bullets don't bounce- off off humans & ... don't even get me started on whatever that is..." said Vinay pointing to the assailant fighting invisible restraints.

Then to my astonishment Vinay pinched himself & then proceeded to pinch me

"Ow!" I yelped in pain.

"Sorry. But I need to ensure that I am awake" Vinay apologized.

"Since it is apparent that I am, the only other explanation is that I am going insane. This is not really happening..."

He was muttering to himself & I was afraid that if he did not snap out of it, he would have a stroke so I did the only thing I could think of... I kissed him.

In that kiss I poured in as much magic as I could to soothe his frayed nerves. For a moment it felt like time had stood still, like this is where we were meant to be, like the past 2 days had never happened. Vinay's arms snaked around me & his lips devoured mine. When he finally pulled away both of us were breathing heavily. Vinay turned to look at the trapped assailant once again then he looked at me. His eyes met mine, a storm of questions begging for answers & then he asked me

"Veena, ... who are you?"

Taking a deep breath, I released a controlled burst of magic towards the trapped man, rendering him unconscious. Vinay had been completely honest with me. He had shared not only the intricacies of his job but also his dreams & aspirations with me. He had opened up about his life, and yet I had kept my own truths hidden. It was time to change that.

"I am a Rakshasi" I announced looking at Vinay.

"My sister, my Nani & my father we are all Rakshasas. My mother too was a Rakshasi. I come from magic though until recently I did not know how to use it. My mother" I paused as a sob unbidden came to my lips. Composing myself I continued "my mother ... was a very powerful Rakshasi. She died when I was a little girl but we do not talk about it. One day she was there waving us goodbye as we left for school & then Baba came to collect us instead of Ma. I still remember the stony façade he sported when he informed us that Ma was no more. Since then, Varsha & I were not allowed to practice magic. Whatever I could do was only things which came naturally to us. Mr. Khanna's murder changed all that. The red mist which I saw was magic Vinay. Mr. Khanna – Mehul was killed by a magical creature"

I had unloaded my whole life story onto Vinay. Now I eagerly looked at him for his reaction. Hoping against hope that he would accept me for who I was. The look on Vinay's face was one of pure shock.

"There is no such thing as Rakshasas Veena. Those are just myths" he said & I realized that his brain had stopped processing anything beyond my announcement of me being a Rakshasi.

"I am a Rakshasi & I have magic Vinay" I reiterated once again. "You have witnessed it right now" I continued "My magic is what alerted me to the danger that Raghu was in & my magic is what saved us right now. I didn't want to tell you because I knew you would not believe me" I said looking at him earnestly "Do you believe me Vinay?" I asked again.

Slowly Vinay walked up to me. He held my face in both his hands & looked into my eyes.

"I believe that you have magic. I have felt it since the day we met. But you can't be a Rakshasi! Rakshasas are evil" he said.

His words were almost like a physical slap. Angry tears unbidden threatened to spill from my eyes.

"Do I look evil to you, Vinay?"

"No. You can never be bad or evil. I know you" said Vinay looking at me in amazement.

"And yet I can assure you that I am a Rakshasi Vinay" I said

"But in all the stories that I have heard which have been passed down through the generations, the rakshasas are always evil... & ugly" Vinay said in a pained voice. He didn't know how to continue.

"And are all the rakshasas always evil Vinay in your stories?" I asked.

"No absolutely not. There are a few good ones even great ones" said Vinay after giving it some thought.

"So why the shock? I could have told you I am a divine being since that would have been easier to digest for you but you asked for honesty, didn't you?" I said moving away from him. "I have told you, my secret. It is now your choice whether to be with me or not"

I needed Vinay to accept me for who I was & I knew I needed to give him time for that. Asking for or demanding anything less wouldn't be fair to either of us.

"That man" I said pointing to the masked man "will be unconscious for the next 2 hrs. You need to get him into police custody & question him. I believe this attack has to do with Mr. Khanna's death-which was by magic & not by any gas or bio weapon. Also, Nemina is a witch & probably the murderer as well though I cannot be sure" I continued deciding to give him the whole truth

"This guy" I said pointing to our assailant lying prone on the ground "will not remember the details of what happened here so you can come up with your own explanation"

"Nemina is a witch???" asked Vinay trying to digest everything that I had told him

"Yes, she is. Though she neither has the hooked nose nor flies around on a broom." I said with a sarcastic smile "That is why the 2 of us could see the magic that killed Mehul in the restaurant"

"Do you know what killed Mehul?" asked Vinay his astonishment evident

"Well, I believe that the entity that killed Mehul & Mrs. Khurana is a Rakta Pishacha- it could also be a witch. But if it is a Rakta pishachi then you need to be careful as they are beings who suck the life force from human beings to prolong their lives & achieve immortality. Maisha looks exactly like her grandmother so she may be one but again I can't say for sure" I replied

"I... I can barely understand what you are implying Veena. But even If I take your words at face value, why would either of them kill Mr. Khanna? For Nemina he was her hen laying golden eggs & he is Maisha's father" exclaimed Vinay.

"You told me that majority of the inheritance of Mr. Khanna goes to Maisha after his death, right?" I asked. Vinay nodded so I continued "As for Nemina, may be Mehul was getting tired of her or maybe she found someone new. In any case the murderer is magical. I thought you should know this" I said as I finally managed to flag down a rickshaw.

"I know it is not easy to believe but that is all I can offer you right now Vinay" I said.

Vinay looked to be deep in thought & did not try to stop me as I got into the rickshaw.

"Don't worry Veena I am not going to tell anyone. Your secret is safe with me," said Vinay.

"I trust you Vinay" I said with a sad smile.

He may be saying it now but once he had enough time to process it, who knows what he would do. Humans are seldom able to fight against inherent biases. But I was still reluctant to use magic on Vinay to modify his memory. That is what Nani had been teaching me the past 2 nights & I was not very good with it. If Vinay & I were to move forward as anything more that friends then he needed to know the truth about me. I waved at him leaving him standing near the masked man a thoughtful look on his face.

After coming home, I narrated the whole episode to Varsha & then to my embarrassment burst out crying. I could still remember the look of shock on Vinay's face & his words that Rakshasas were evil. Though I had held myself not letting his words affect me, they had hurt immensely. In my naivety, I had imagined Vinay to be different from others – more accepting. I had convinced myself that since he had experienced the burden of expectations from his own family, he would be cognizant of the labels that society places on people or on races. But perhaps I was mistaken. Perhaps Vinay & I were never meant for the long haul.

In our family it was not a necessity to marry only a rakshasa. In fact, cross breeding was encouraged especially for females. Male Rakshasas were fewer in number & most of them were chauvinists believing the place of females was in the bed or in the kitchen. There were few exceptions like my father but overall, it was better for Rakshasis to marry men. The magic flowed more naturally in the female line & was honed better without the aggression & the ego associated with the males. Most of the Rakshasis married to humans kept their powers hidden & their partners were never aware of it. In case they had sons, most were non-magical – just like my father. If there was a daughter born who manifested early, the Rakshasi's covered to the best of their abilities. Besides humans like Vinay, were wired such that they would rather believe in a whole lot of coincidences & fate than magic. So far there had been no problems.

But I had wanted something different. I wanted a true life-partner who would not only accept me for who I was but who would be my strongest supporter. When I met Vinay, I had thought he would be the one. Varsha was angry on hearing Vinay's opinions on Rakshasas.

"He doesn't deserve you di. Just Forget him!" she said.

That night I practiced magic with a renewed sense of purpose.

"Nani, today there was one more death. I think the Rakta Pishacha is getting desperate. Don't you think you should teach me to perfect my magical attacks?" I asked.

I did not want to just shield myself if there was a second attack. I wanted to go on the offensive

"You have no patience girl" said Nani "Had you paid more attention when you were kids, you girls would have been better at attacks by now" She smiled looking at the worried looks on mine & Varsha's faces

"Don't worry girls. That Pishacha will not be able to harm you. You just need to unleash your magic the way you did that day in school. Use the white magic that I taught you girl- at the haunted cottage" she winked.

We practiced till midnight with each of us taking turns attacking the other. At one point Nani & Varsha combined their magic & attacked me. When I was successfully able to repel that attack, Nani seemed to be satisfied & gave me permission to go to sleep.

Chapter 24 – Dark Musings

Finally, the stage was set. All pawns were in place. All that remained was for me to make my last move. I fully intended to enjoy the windfall that had fallen in my lap. Threatening Veena had not worked. She was definitely stringer that I had thought earlier. Not just magically but even in spirit. It was something I found admirable even in an enemy. The sheer brilliance of Veena's soul would sustain me, rejuvenate me. I was sure of it. Her magic while strong was still dormant - making me sure of my victory.

My escape plan was already in motion. I had made certain that no one would be able to follow the money trail. Disappearing was becoming increasingly difficult in these times with the numerous mechanisms put in place for tracking people. But there were still places I knew. Places which no human would be able to access - where I could hide. I would stay there till I became a distant memory for all who knew me in this avatar. That is one of the perks of being immortal. The people who knew me would grow old & die. The only thing I needed to do was to wait it out. While tedious, this could be managed with enough money.

It would be easy to lure her into my trap because unlike others typical of her kind, her soul was still tethered to this plane, this place. What kept her tied were the golden threads of love & relationships, her family & people she considered her friends. But these threads also made her vulnerable. I would have to ensure that she was isolated from her family for though their magic was not as strong, they would be an unwanted distraction for which I did not have time. By the time they realized what was happening, I would be long gone. I gave a small smile of satisfaction as I once again gazed in my mirror.

Mrs. Khurana had put up quite a fight even after the breath had left her body. I had to exert every ounce of my magic to devour her soul. I went through the plan once again to ensure that there would be no loose threads. If everything else failed, I would be able to use Veena's emotions against her as had been clearly demonstrated when her sorrow brought down her shield. Feeling confident, I dialed the number that would put the final part of my plan into action.

Chapter 25 – The trap

The next morning, I woke up to my mobile ringing. I rubbed my eyes & glanced at the screen to see Vinay's name flashing on the screen. I felt a moment of pure joy but tamped down my feelings.

"Hello" I said tentatively

"Oh, thank God! you answered. I need your help" said Vinay without any preamble. "Its Nemina she wants to meet us at the same chai ki tapri at precisely 12pm today. She said she has new information pertaining to the case. Will you come with me?"

I found this quite weird. What new information could she have now? I was not yet convinced of Nemina's guilt but her claim of new information pertaining to the case struck me as peculiar, and my instincts tingled with unease. And why was she so adamant about having me along this time too? I couldn't shake the feeling that there was more to her request than met the eye- or ear in this case.

My gut feeling pushed me to take action. I decided to go to Nemina's house before the designated time to confirm my suspicions. I took a hurried shower & had my morning cup of coffee grabbing 2 toasts on the way out. No one at home had woken up yet so I left a note. I rode my scooty to the colony of row houses & parked it out of sight behind a tree. I slowly made my way to Nemina's house. Row house number 13- most appropriate for a witch. I huddled in the shadows next to the open window I had noticed the first time around.

Floral linen drapes of a pale blue color hung from an ornate curtain rod. A sideboard cabinet held the photo of a smiling girl who had protectively placed her arm around a younger boy. I could easily recognize Nemina from the photo. The boy looked like a younger version of the teenager who had called Nemina the first time we met- Nimish, her brother. Suddenly I heard shuffling of feet & Nemina's voice. She was speaking with someone on her mobile.

"Yes, I had called Vinay. No, she will come. I am quite sure she will. If she doesn't, I will go to her house & make up another story. No!

you have to give me time till noon. That is what we had agreed on. I will get her to the warehouse. Now let me speak to Nimish. Please I beg of you. He is just a boy. I will get you Veena, just have patience." Then she hung up & I could see tears in her eyes.

As the full implications of the conversation hit me, I realized that Nemina was not acting on her own but her actions were being dictated by someone else. She was bargaining with that someone - on the other end of the phone line, promising to deliver Vinay and me in exchange for her brother's safety. A surge of empathy washed over me as I understood her torment. Her brother's life was on the line, and if it was the Rakta Pishacha who had taken him, he had limited time. I couldn't turn my back on her, not when she was facing a situation so dire. The pieces fell into place—the meeting at the Tapri was meant to be a trap for me. But if played right, Nemina and I could work together to rescue her brother. As I slipped away from Nemina's house, a plan began to formulate in my mind. I needed to ensure that Nimish's life was spared. That the Pishacha did not feed again.

"Thank you for coming" said Nemina as soon as Vinay & I entered the Tapri.

We had come together on his bike. After hearing the one-sided conversation at Nemina's house, I had called Vinay. We had met at my office & come up with a tentative plan to rescue Nemina's brother. The problem was going to be to communicate it to Nemina without the kidnapper being aware of our intentions. I had already gathered that the kidnapper would not completely trust Nemina. While entering the tapri, I had noticed 2 men seemingly out for a smoke keeping a watch on the girl. This confirmed my suspicions. Nemina also seemed to know their purpose & kept glancing nervously at them through the corner of her eyes. I would have only one chance to accomplish what I wanted to convey through magic & hope that she got the message. As we sat down, I willed Nemina to look at me.

"I have asked Neetu to make you the same special tea that you had ordered last time" said Nemina as she kept looking down playing with the ends of her dupatta refusing to meet my eyes.

She was making this more difficult. As the steaming cups of tea were brought out by Neetu who herself seemed tense, I grabbed Nemina's hand beneath the table. Startled, she looked up at me. I was attempting something different- something that I had not tried before. Rather than reading her thoughts, I was trying to project my thoughts into her brain. At first, she resisted but when I indicated with my eyes towards the 2 men outside, she lowered her mental barriers & allowed me in. Our plan was simple - to go along with Nemina & get entry to the warehouse. After that it would all be down to beating the Rakta Pishacha. I was quite confident that once we were in her territory & she felt like she had the upper hand, the muscle would be dispatched.

The tea was drugged. That was the first thought I picked up on from Nemina. I communicated that we would pretend to drink the drugged tea. As Vinay was about to drink the tea, I nudged him with my foot & indicated to the tea. Since Vinay possessed no magic, I was unable to communicate with him the way I was with Nemina. However, the foot nudge seemed to work. He quietly poured out his tea on the floor beneath the table & raised the empty cup to his lips. I gave a small imperceptible nod. I followed suit. Then both of us promptly pretended to be unconscious. Now it was up to Nemina. She would have to use her magic to convince the 2 goons outside that we were indeed unconscious.

When I opened my eyes next, I saw that I was inside the godown & that my hands were tied. We had to co-operate to get our hands tied to get into the dark Maruti van which had transported us here. As I had suspected the goons were immediately asked to leave, once they had us securely tied to chairs. But I had yet to recognize who the muffled voice belonged to- it was definitely female as it barked out crisp instructions on what was to be done with us. I had kept my eyes shut not wanting to give away that I was not unconscious but the Rakta Pishacha must have suspected something for once we were tied, I could feel magic being poured into the normal rope bindings. Not strong enough to not be broken but it would take time.

The LED bulb hanging in the center of a narrow space was the only source of illumination. As I looked around, I saw that Nemina was also tied to a chair on my right & Vinay on my left. I was surprised to find Mehul's ghost standing in one corner of the room looking at me with keen eyes. Besides the ghost was one more chair. There was one more person tied to that chair as well.

"Is that you Pinky" I called.

"No, you idiot. Why would she be tied to a chair?" an angry voice answered.

"Maisha...but then who...?" before I could finish my sentence Pinky walked into the room on her heels.

"Never thought it could be dumb old Pinky, right?" she asked with a mocking laugh. "I gave you so many clues to think it was Maisha why would you think it was anyone but her?"

"You... you are a Rakta Pishacha! It was you who killed your husband & the nanny & tried to end Raghu's life as well" I asked in surprise.

Chapter 26 – Immortality

"Yes, you guessed right," said Pinky. "Kudos to you little girl for figuring out what I am. But what are you going to do about it?" She asked "Do you really think you can finish me or that your boyfriend here can?" She pointed to Vinay who was watching the whole scene unfold with a mixture of wonder & horror on his face.

"You should never have gotten involved in this Veena. Humans fear us or they abhor us. Isn't that right Nemina?" She looked to the young girl who was struggling against the ropes binding her. Nemina gave her a hateful glare.

"Where is my brother?" asked Nemina "I don't see him here. If anything happens to him, I will kill you"

"Oh my! So much love for that child. I have kept him at another location with my 'son'. Don't worry he is well & will stay so as long as I get her" said Pinky pointing to me. Her face had morphed into a mask of condescension

"So, you know Nemina is a witch, do you?" I asked stalling for time. I knew with a bit more time, I would be able to free myself of the magical ropes.

"Oh! I know what she is but I still can't figure out what you are" said Pinky "Had you not been in that restaurant, perhaps I would never have longed for your soul." She continued looking at me hungrily.

"She is a Rakshasi!" yelled Nemina with a gleeful look.

"Shut up blabbermouth. You think she is going to give you a golden star for telling her that? She already knows I am a paranormal. If you had simply told me your suspicions instead of trying your cute helpless college girl routine on Vinay then we wouldn't be here." I said angrily.

"And how was I supposed to know that you of all people would believe me? I thought you would assume that I was accusing her out of jealousy. Besides I was myself not sure if it was her or Maisha" retorted Nemina.

"Like I would kill my own father! I don't know what my father saw in you. It was certainly not your brains" said Maisha from the other end of the room.

"Didn't I deduce that you were a witch? Shouldn't that have given you a clue that I knew about the paranormal world?" I said to Nemina "And as for you Maisha" I continued "You were angry with everyone all the time. I can understand that may be that was your way to deal with your grief but you played right into her hands"

Nemina nodded considering my words.

"Too bad either of you couldn't recognize what my dear mother is though - step-mother," said Maisha.

"Oh! don't be silly dear. These 2 girls can barely cloak their magic. It's like they are broadcasting to any paranormal around. I have been around for a long time to know that is not wise. They would never have been able to recognize what I am" Pinky said smiling slyly.

"You are a really old lady. That's what you are. We get it" said Nemina making a face. "As for you Veena, maybe I should have confided in you. But you should have seen Vinay's face when we started talking about red mists & bio weapons. He did not even consider how absurd it sounded. Better science than magic. You know about paranormals but your boyfriend definitely has his reservations." she said.

"Vinay is not my boyfriend. We have just been on a few dates. In fact, we are not even together anymore" I said in a choked voice glancing at Vinay who still seemed unable to fully comprehend the scene.

"Really I thought you guys were seriously in love the way he kept ignoring me," said Pinky

"He doesn't go after overly made-up sluts" I said as Vinay finally snapped out & grinned at me.

"We will see about that won't we now" said Pinky as she circled around Vinay's chair. "Once I wipe certain parts of his memory, he will not only be completely in love with me but will also convince the police of how these 2 – she pointed to Maisha & Nemina plotted to murder my husband for money & how he had to kill them in self-defense."

"And what about me?" I asked.

"You would have died a tragic heroes death trying to protect me- the beautiful widow from these 2 murderers"

"You can't just kill them all" said Vinay "The police will never believe that story"

"Obviously they won't. But she thinks she can seduce any man to believe her version of the truth. The past 5 years I have seen her flirting with everyone from grandpa's doctor to our lawyer to even the gardener. She has no class!" said Maisha.

"Enough" yelled Pinky. "Is this how you want to spend your last moments in this world? Throwing insults at me you pathetic little girls?" she said angrily

"Hey who are you calling pathetic? Let me tell you I have a very interesting life. I am young & not hitched to a middle-aged pudgy man" said Nemina bragging.

"Yeah! her life is so much better than yours – at least she didn't have to marry a guy 15 years her senior & a widower at that," said Maisha.

I could now understand the anger that Maisha had for her step mother.

"Are you sure making her angry is the best way to handle this?" whispered Vinay.

I could see that he was quite amused with the conversation.

"What does it matter? She intends to kill us either way." I replied.

"Obviously you are right. But don't you want to know why am I killing people?" asked Pinky me hearing our conversation.

"Not really. But for the un-initiated, that is you – Maisha & Vinay; Pinky is what most people know as a Rakta Pishacha which means she sucks the life force of others to prolong her life. I believe it is Pinky who killed your mother Maisha after she met Mehul & decided that this is the life she wanted" I said looking sympathetically at Maisha "After that you have managed to suck the life force of only one other person – one of Mehul's former clients Mr. Subramanium." I said to Pinky.

I had uncovered this bit from the information Vinay had gathered.

"If you recall Vinay, Mr. T. Subramanium first suffered a paralytic stroke after making his will & then died in the hospital. I guess Pinky here got greedy there & tapped him again instead of risking a new victim & in the process the poor guy lost his life" I concluded.

"O he willingly came to me" said Pinky "You see he was in love with me. Even in the hospital when he was dying, he professed his undying love" Pinky laughed without any mirth. It was a dead laugh & chilled me to my very bones.

"But my dad wasn't in love with you anymore. He had started realizing what you were. That is why you decided to kill him. I have heard enough of your fights so don't even try to convince me otherwise" interrupted Maisha

"What about Mehul? Didn't she suck his soul too?" asked Vinay going to the more basic questions. Since he was new to the whole magic thing, I was sure he would have a lot of questions.

"No. Mehul is here now. His ghost is standing in the corner there" I said pointing to the corner where the ghost was waiting with a forlorn expression.

Everyone was astonished at my announcement including Pinky.

"So, you can see ghosts?" asked Maisha "How is he? How is my father?"

"Mehul is feeling very repentant. Pinky was not able to feed on his soul though she did kill him. Mehul's ghost was trapped here – I believe by Pinky so that he could not warn me about her identity."

"I knew you could see him the moment I saw your reaction in the restaurant. After failing to feed on Raghu, I saw you talking to his ghost. Imagine my shock – I wanted to trap a witch but found a Rakshasi instead! Lucky me!" Pinky gave that chilling laugh again.

"But why was she unable to feed on Mehul?" Vinay asked again.

"I think it again boils down to what Nemina did" I looked to her for confirmation. "I think Pinky had to use other means to kill Mehul because he already suspected what she was. She hasn't been able to absorb his life essence but she did manage to trap his ghost else he would have told us the truth" I said. The look Pinky shot me told me I was correct.

"I really did care for Mehul. After Mehul told me his suspicions, I tried to warn him to stay away from her but he wanted eternal life for both of us... he had decided to blackmail Pinky. So, I gave him the symbol which would protect him should she ever try to feed on him" said Nemina with moist eyes.

"But it didn't save his life" I concluded & she nodded.

"So, in short - she needs to feed now. But why trap you specifically?" asked Vinay curious.

"Because I am a Rakshasi & Nemina is a witch & Pinky believes that the life force of a witch & a Rakshasi will sustain her for longer." I said.

"Very good class" said Pinky clapping her hands.

"You being a Rakshasi has now given me a choice. So - who goes first. The witch or the Rakshasi." Said Pinky rubbing her hands.

"This was never part of the deal" yelled Nemina "You had promised you would let me go if I got you Veena"

"And you obviously know how trustworthy is a Rakta Pishacha" I couldn't help but chime in

Pinky veered towards me eyeing me closely.

"You seem more interesting Veena. I can sense your magic but I would never have guessed you to be a Rakshasi. There is a bit of Rakshasi in you but there is also something else. You are like a cocktail of many things that ideally shouldn't mix together but have somehow managed to in your case." She said circling me

"But before that aren't you going to tell us how you became a Rakta Pishacha?" asked Maisha.

I recognized her desperate delay tactic & played along.

"Yes, I would also like to know. All I know is that humans become Pishachas when they have a thirst for revenge which consumes them" I said.

"Very well then. Let me tell you my story," said Pinky triumphantly.

"I am not interested in your story so can you cover my ears" asked Nemina

"Shut up witch. It will be better for you if you don't get me angry," said Pinky.

"Oh, you just want an audience that is how old people are" said Nemina "they just want to talk but no one wants to listen to them. I think you love the sound of your own voice" She rolled her eyes.

"I am not old & I can't take one more minute of you talking" said Pinky as she took out a roll of duct tape. My magical bindings had weakened a lot in the interim but I was not yet free.

"If you talk again, I will tape up your mouths – all of you" said Pinky "I will tell my story & you will listen" she continued.

"Very Many years ago I lived in a village with my husband. The times were different then or perhaps they were the same for I have heard echoes of my story through the generations that have come after me..." said Pinky or the Rakta Pishacha with a determined look.

"My husband was not happy with me as I was unable to bear his children. All the women in the village also avoided me & called me names. I still put up with it because I had nowhere else to go. One day after a petty argument, my husband hit me on my head with a boulder. When I lost consciousness, instead of taking me to a doctor, he threw me in the river. Fortunately for me a stranger saw me being thrown & rescued me when my husband had left. When I regained consciousness, I wanted to get revenge on my husband for what he had done. The stranger who had rescued me gave me this book" Pinky took out a small book from her purse which had the same symbol I had seen in the portrait of Maisha's grandmother.

"As you can guess, the stranger was a Pishacha. He had initially wanted to feed on me but looking at my beauty he was overcome with lust & he decided to make me like him so that I could become his companion. After my transformation was complete, the first person I killed was the stranger who had changed me. I did not wish to be bound to anyone in my new life. Then I killed my husband & all the ladies who were ever mean to me" said Pinky glancing in mirror & smiling. "It has been so easy for me to trap men. They all think I am some naïve girl & are falling over themselves to take care of me" again she gave a mirthless laugh. Then looking at me she said "And now it is your turn to nourish me"

"That was a pathetic story. You should never tell it to anyone. After all that happened to you, you have also ended up killing a lot of innocent people. No one here is going to feel any sympathy listening to your story now." I said "I bet you got that photo of Maisha's grandmother doctored to show the symbol & what about Sanish? He isn't your biological child, is he?" I asked

"Figured it all out, have you? Yes, I used photo shop for that photo. As for Sanish, I convinced Mehul that we needed a surrogate & then bribed her for her eggs"

"But what about the handkerchiefs?" I asked.

"What handkerchiefs?" asked Pinky confused "There were no handkerchiefs- are you delusional?"

"I found a handkerchief at the haunted cottage behind Glocal Juntion when Vinay & I had gone exploring" I said looking at Nemina & Maisha. "The handkerchief had a skull embroidered in the corner like you two carry"

"What do you mean both of us?" asked Maisha "Those handkerchiefs were custom made for me by my father. He understood my morbid tastes." She smiled at the memory while Mr. Khanna's ghost looked at me guiltily.

"Mehul gave me the hanky when something got stuck in my eye. It was the first lot he had gotten made for Maisha & I liked the design as well so he gave me a half dozen of them" said Nemina haughtily

"You really are disgusting father!" Maisha said angrily "I hope he can hear me?" she asked looking to me to which I nodded.

"But why was it at the cottage?" asked Vinay

"Because I followed these 2 lovebirds that day to the restaurant," said Maisha

"What!" exclaimed Mr. Khanna's ghost finally breaking his silence. "Why were you spying on me?" he asked

"She can't hear you" I told Mr. Khanna. Then I relayed his message to Maisha

"Because I didn't want you to make a terrible mistake & marry this one as well," said Maisha with tears in her eyes

"I hate you Pinky" spat the ghost as he tried to pat Maisha's head fondly.

Suddenly Maisha looked up in astonishment. "Is he touching me?" she asked & I could see the vulnerable teenager behind the angry mask. One who desperately missed her father. However, he may have been I was happy to know that Mehul had been a good father. I nodded at Maisha. The action was not lost on Pinky.

"I hate you too darling" said Pinky to the ghost "That was a nice family reunion. Now enough talk. I am going to kill you first

Rakshasi" saying this Pinky raised here hands unleashing the red mist on me.

Things happened really fast after that. I got up from the chair & kicked it to the side having finally freed myself of the magical bindings. Pinky only laughed as the mist changed direction & started moving towards me. I put up the shield like I was taught. Pinky watched in wonder as the mist tried to break through the shield & failed. It dissipated after a few tries. Pinky gave an anguished cry & lashed out with more magic. This was not like the mist it was burning red & clashed with the magical shield I had thrown destroying it. Pinky laughed like a maniac. I was feeling helpless but then I looked at the other people trapped in the room with me who were at the mercy of a blood thirsty Pishacha - I was their only hope.

I closed my eyes & summoned all my magic. The emotions in my heart channeling the energy. I imitated the motions I had seen Nani perform in our first lesson. When Pinky released the second blast of her red magic, I opened my eyes & to my astonishment when I saw my reflection in the glass nearby, I could see that my eyes were once again burning bright yellow. Pinky's magic collided with my burst of magic. While hers burned red, mine was a flash of bright white. The two streams collided with the white one slowly pushing back the red till it was completely destroyed. Then the white magic engulfed Pinky who screamed just once before completely disappearing. All that remained was a pile of crumpled clothes on the floor. A minute or two passed in complete silence as I stood rooted to my spot. The silence was shattered by Vinay's voice.

"Where did she go? Did she just disappear?" Vinay asked from behind me looking at the clothes pile.

"She should never have existed in the physical realm" said Nemina as she got up from the chair pulling away the duct tape from her mouth.

She too seemed to have broken through the magical restraints.

"She is where she should have been very many years ago" she continued.

She mutely went to the corner to free Maisha. As for me, I was just tired after expending so much of magic.

"I trust you will be able to wrap this up from here on Mr. Verma. I have a ghost to help" I said without looking at Vinay as I walked to the corner of the room where the ghost was trying to communicate with Maisha & Nemina.

Epilogue

It had been over 2 weeks since my showdown with the Rakta Pishacha. I had helped Mr. Khanna's ghost to say good bye to his daughter, his son, his father & to his beloved Nemina. Though in unlikely circumstances Mehul & Nemina did really seem to care about one another. After that, Mehul wanted to visit all places which held meaning to him in his mortal life & had asked me for a day. I had met him the next day morning at the gate of our bungalow & then helped him to cross over into the afterlife with the help of my Nani. I was apparently capable enough to do it on my own but had never had the opportunity to learn how to do it. Nani said she would include it in the next lesson.

Mrs. Joshi who I believed had seen the ghostly ritual would spread even more gossip in the colony now that she had seen me wave my hands about like a magician. Perhaps she would assume I was participating in one more talent show or that it was a new dance form – in any case I did not have the time to be bothered about her. I had made my peace with who I was now & the time of hiding was long past gone. The media had already convicted Pinky of Mr. Khanna's murder after the police named her as the prime suspect. Vinay had released a statement that Pinky had used slow poison to kill her husband so that she could take control of his estate. Since it was an herbal poison, it had been difficult to trace. She had also planned to challenge the will in court & since both the children were minors & there was no pre-nuptial agreement signed, she would probably have succeeded. Nemina had also given her statement that Mehul had confided in her about his wife wanting to kill him & she had gone into hiding after his death fearing for her life. It was assumed that Pinky's original plan had been to kill Nemina & Maisha but she got scared after the police suspicion was directed at her & ran away. Whatever happened to Raghu was probably age related & nothing to do with the murder. He was doing well now & had no recollection of the incident at all.

A red alert was issued for Mrs. Pinky Khanna but obviously she would never be found & though there were quite a few loose ends, no one was questioning the police. My presence at the godown had not been announced. Everyone had agreed that it would be better this way.

Vinay & I had not spoken in the aftermath of what happened. I think it was too hard for him to get over the fact that he had fallen for a Rakshasi & that not only was magic real - it was also dangerous. My father's firm had managed to trace the money trail after I gave the diary I had recovered from Pinky to my father & that had saved the house of the Khannas. In the absence of Pinky, all the property of Mr. Khanna would now go to his legal heirs i.e his daughter & his son. I believed that Maisha had learned her lesson & would take care of the Sr. Mr. Khanna for whatever else may have been her motivations, Maisha did not look like the kind of girl who would leave her grandfather at an old age home. Post Pinky now she was looking forward to being a part of Pune's high society & for that to happen she needed to stay in the good books of all. Besides she had just turned 18 & needed supervision which I was sure her grandfather would happily provide.

On the work front, the Poonawala project had given me the breakthrough I wanted & I had already got 2 contracts on which the work would begin soon.

Nemina had contacted me after some days & we had managed to forge an acquaintance of some sort. She planned to use her brains rather than her looks to make her way forward in life & was currently looking for a job. She was also working on her magic to enable her to recognize & fight against a paranormal enemy.

I occasionally thought about Vinay in moments of loneliness but as Varsha said if he couldn't accept me for who I was then we did not have a future. The magic lessons with my Nani were continuing & now Varsha was also a regular participant. If anything, this entire incident had taught me that we were certainly not alone in the paranormal world & it was always better to stay prepared.

Every day I was spending time in Ma's library learning from Tantrika Yogini & practicing magic. My Nani had planned for an official initiation ceremony for Varsha & I into the magic world as adults. It was a ceremony I was looking forward to. After all who knew what the future would hold for a Rakshasi...

Acknowledgements

I want to thank everyone who took the time out to read my book. If you liked it, please take a few minutes & leave a review. Reviews are definitely helpful & motivating for independent authors like me.

A big thank you to my brother, Nikhil Thakur for his genuine & infectious enthusiasm for the story. Thanks to my friend & fitness trainer Shivani Vig for bringing Rakshasi to life in the lovely illustration on the cover. Finally, loads of thanks to my husband Devdatta Potnis for all his inputs which have gone to make this story much better (in my opinion).

www.ingramcontent.com/pod-product-compliance
Lightning Source LLC
LaVergne TN
LVHW041203150826
845673LV00001B/274

9798891339668